HIS FORBIDDEN DIAMOND

HIS FORBIDDEN DIAMOND

BY

SUSAN STEPHENS

First published in Great Britain 2014
by Mills & Boon, an imprint of Harlequin (UK) Limited,
Large Print edition 2014
Eton House, 18-24 Paradise Road,
Richmond, Surrey, TW9 1SR

ISBN: 978-0-263-24127-3

Harlequin (UK) Limited's policy is to use papers that are natural, renewable and recyclable products and made from wood grown in sustainable forests. The logging and manufacturing processes conform to the legal environmental regulations of the country of origin.

Printed and bound in Great Britain
by CPI Antony Rowe, Chippenham, Wiltshire

For Laurie, who, like all the best heroines,
is smart and fun, with an unshakeable
determination to get the very best out of me.

CHAPTER ONE

TYR SKAVANGA IS HOME!

THE HEADLINE BLARED at him. His sister Britt had placed the newspaper on her desk, where she knew he couldn't fail to see it. Britt was trying to tell him in her usual no-nonsense way how much he'd been missed, and how words could never express his three sisters' happiness now he'd returned. The photograph beneath the headline showed Britt, Eva and Leila, hugging each other, their faces wreathed in smiles of joy.

Because of him.

Turning, he went to stare out of Britt's office window, where snow drifted from a black sky like frozen sighs. Everything outside the building was pristine white and unspoiled, while inside, reflected in the window, was a killer's face, *his face*, and he couldn't hide from that.

He had no wish to, Tyr thought grimly. He was back in Skavanga, the small mining town that bore his family's name, to reboot himself amongst people he loved. He'd stayed away for too long after leaving the army, to protect his sisters and friends from a man who was vastly changed. Britt, his eldest sister, had never given up on him, never ceased trying to contact him whether he replied to her messages or not. *Not being the usual response from him.* Britt was one of the few people who could reach him through her husband, Sheikh Sharif. Sharif was one of Tyr's closest friends and had remained loyal throughout, refusing to reveal Tyr's whereabouts, or what he was doing while he was away, even to his wife, Britt.

In the end it was a child who had pricked his conscience and brought him back. He had carried the little girl from the war zone to reunite her with her family in a refugee camp, and when the tears of joy subsided she had turned to him to ask, with all the concern a child of seven who'd seen too much could muster:

'Don't you have a family, Mr Tyr?'

The little girl's question had shamed him, shattered him. It had broken through his armour, forcing him to think about those he'd left behind. Yes, he had a family and he loved them very much, he had explained to her. No one in the girl's family had commented when his eyes filled with tears. They'd seen everything. They were reunited. They were alive. That was all they asked for. When he'd left the camp to return to the desert to begin rebuilding, he'd worked until his strength gave out, and all the time he was there the little girl's comment about his family nagged at him, made him realise how lucky he was to have people who loved him. He knew then he had to go home, though he had dreaded confronting his sisters, who would see through the shell in an instant to this new and much changed man.

He had been of inestimable value to Special Forces, a senior officer had told him as he pinned a medal on Tyr's chest, but that wasn't something Tyr wanted carved on his tombstone. He wanted to be remembered for what he'd built, and not for what he'd destroyed. He'd encountered three types of soldier in battle: those who enjoyed their job, those who went about their duty with unfailing courage and loyalty to comrades and country, and those who would never recover from what they'd seen, physically, mentally, or both. He had no excuse. He was strong. He had the love of a good family, and somehow he had managed, not just to stay alive, but to remain relatively unharmed, at least outwardly. And now it was up to him to complete the healing process so he could be of some use to those less fortunate than himself.

'Tyr!'

'Britt.' He swung round just in time for his beautiful sister to throw herself into his arms. Britt's face was ecstatic, but she was full of questions. Flight good? Journey good?

'You look great, Tyr.'

His mouth quirked. 'Liar.'

His eldest sister took a step back to take a proper look at him. 'Okay, so your clothes look great.'

'Better,' he said dryly as they shared a laugh. 'I stopped off in Milan, knowing if I was coming to a party hosted by my glamorous sisters, I had better look the part.'

Britt's face grew concerned. 'You know, you don't have to do anything you don't want to, Tyr.'

'But I want to be here. I wanted to come home and see you.'

'So, you're ready to face the music?' Britt enquired, glancing across the road to the town's smartest hotel, where she had arranged a welcome home party for him.

'I am if you are.'

'I only wish we had longer to talk, but you've never been one to ease yourself into a situation by degrees, have you, Tyr?'

'Full immersion,' he confirmed, determined to keep the tone upbeat. 'It's the only way I know.'

Britt gave a disbelieving hum. 'If you say so.'

'I do say so.' He gestured towards the hotel, where they could see cars arriving. 'And thank you for going to all this trouble for me.'

She laughed. 'It's nice to have the chance. And if I can't welcome the town's hero home…'

'Just welcome your brother home. That's all I want.'

'I'd go to the ends of the earth for you, Tyr—and almost had to,' Britt reminded him wryly.

'Those emails kept coming,' he agreed.

'And you kept ignoring them.'

'But I saved you a trip in the end,' he pointed out.

'Tyr, you never change.' Britt was laughing but her eyes were sad behind the fixed smile because they both knew that was a lie. He'd changed a whole lot.

'This quiet time in my office has been good for you, though, hasn't it, Tyr?'

'This quiet time has been perfect. Thank you, Britt.'

Aside from shopping for some essentials, which meant ditching the desert boots and safari shirts in favour of city clothes, Tyr hadn't suffered any human contact since leaving the sandbox. After the silence of the desert even street noise was deafening. But when could Britt not face anything that came her way? he reflected as he gazed into the eyes of a most admirable woman. Even if she hadn't been his sister, he would have placed Britt on a pedestal a mile high.

'Well, you've had your moment,' she told him briskly. 'I want a few words alone with you, and then we'll go.'

He frowned. 'This sounds serious.'

'There's a lot to tell you, Tyr. You've been away for such a long time. Leila's had twins—'

'This I know—you already told me.'

'I told you when they were born,' Britt agreed. 'They're practically school age now, yet you still haven't seen them.'

He acknowledged this with a regretful dip of his head.

'And Leila's pregnant again—'

'What?' This was news to him. 'Raffa doesn't waste any time.'

'Stop with the dinosaur spiel. Those two adore each other. They want a football team, according to Leila. And if you will go off radar the world isn't going to stand still until you decide to come back.'

Where he'd been there was no communication with the outside world—not until he set that communication up and moved on, leaving others to go about the business of contacting loved ones. For a long time he'd been too beat up inside to even think about inflicting himself on his sisters.

'You're not going to tell me where you were, are you, Tyr?'

'Need-to-know basis only.' He made light of it and shrugged. His work was important to him. It was the only way he knew to make reparation. He didn't want to talk about that work to anyone, not even to Britt. He didn't want praise for putting right the wrong he'd done. He just wanted to get on with the job.

Britt shook her head at him. 'Well, I give up. But just wait until you see Leila. She looks—'

'Huge?' he suggested, ducking as Britt aimed a swipe at him.

And just like that they were back to the happy days, the carefree days. 'So, what else is going on I should know about?'

'Jazz is here.'

Electricity coursed through him. 'Jazz. I haven't seen Jazz for years.' Just the mention of Sharif's younger sister's name took him back to wild school holidays, when he could ride himself into the ground and swim until his arms ached, and think of nothing more but the next harmless adventure with his two friends from Kareshi. But beneath Britt's matter-of-fact tone, he sensed something more. 'So?' He shrugged. 'What's happening with Jazz?' He was fairly confident Sharif would have told him if anything serious had happened to his Jazz—Princess Jasmina of Kareshi, as Jazz was better known to the world. 'Jazz is okay, isn't she?'

'Of course she is.'

'But?' He played it down, but his heart had stopped at the thought of harm coming to Jazz. They'd known each other since Sharif had first invited Tyr to spend his school holidays in Kareshi, where Jazz teased him unmercifully for his lack of desert lore. He'd shrugged the irritating kid sister off, but surprised himself by always being pleased to see her. A type of camaraderie had grown between them, and the thought of Jazz sick, or injured— His stomach churned. He'd seen too much of that.

'But nothing, Tyr,' Britt insisted. 'I'd tell you if there was anything wrong.'

He searched Britt's eyes, knowing that wasn't the whole story.

'She's coming tonight, Tyr.'

'Great.' It would be good to see Jazz, though

Sharif's sister could see through everyone, and he wasn't sure how he felt about that.

'She's changed, Tyr,' Britt said quietly.

He looked up.

'Like the rest of us, Tyr, Jazz has grown up.'

What was his sister trying to tell him? He shrugged, picturing Jazz with braces and pig-tails. How much could one person change? He glanced at his reflection in the window, where he got his answer to that.

'What's wrong, Tyr?'

He slanted a smile. 'Nothing. Absolutely nothing's wrong.'

'We've all changed,' Britt said, reading him easily, 'but at least you're smiling now. Thinking of Jazz?'

He hummed and shrugged Britt's question off, but he was thinking about Jazz, who, all those years back, had used to refer to him as the guy from the frozen north with the funny name. Sharif, Jazz and he had been an oddball team. Jazz started out the most unwanted member of that team, but she was also the most determined, and could ride him and Sharif into the ground. And she knew the shifting patterns of the desert like the back of her hand. There had been no getting away from Jazz Kareshi, so in the end they'd given up.

'Don't look so worried, Britt. I can handle Jazz,' he said with confidence.

'Just don't tease her, Tyr.'

'Don't tease Jazz?' He frowned. Jazz had always been the butt of their humour, and Jazz had always given back as good as she got.

'Jazz has only agreed to come tonight because this is such a big family occasion. And I'm here to chaperone her,' Britt added with a meaningful look. 'Me and Sharif, that is.'

He frowned. 'This is all sounding terribly formal and not a bit like Jazz.'

'Like I said, Tyr, Jazz is all grown up, and unmarried sisters of the ruling sheikh in Kareshi don't share our freedoms.'

'Is Sharif penning her in?'

'Don't be silly. You know Sharif is a big advocate for progress. This is Jazz's decision, and we have to respect her for her beliefs. It shows a quiet strength and lots of courage, in my opinion. Jazz has stood by Sharif's side throughout as he's coaxed Kareshi into the twenty-first century, and now she doesn't want to do anything to rock the boat, let alone give the traditionalists in Kareshi an excuse to criticise Sharif for implementing progress too quickly.'

'So Jazz sacrifices herself?' he demanded, outraged. 'Jazz shuts herself away?'

'Not exactly, but Jazz has become quite conservative, so for her sake, Tyr, just tone it down when you see her, okay?'

'What do you think I'm going to do? We've been friends for most of our lives, Britt. I'm hardly going to leap on her.'

'Just cool the friendship, and stay clear of Jazz, except for the most perfunctory greeting. Okay?'

He raked his hair. 'I can't believe you're serious. Is anyone allowed to approach the royal presence?'

'Don't mock her, Tyr. Of course they are.' Britt fired a warning glance across his bows for making light of something that was obviously a great concern to her. 'Jazz lives a near normal life in Kareshi. Sharif broke all the traditionalists' rules by giving Jazz a job at his racing stables, where she's excelled in management, but, more importantly, this has opened the floodgates for all the women of Kareshi to work, if they choose to do so.'

'But?' he prompted, homing in on Britt's brief hesitation.

'But it's made Jazz more determined than ever to uphold tradition in other areas of her life, so that no one can find fault with Sharif's decision to allow her to work.'

'What does "upholding tradition" mean exactly?'

'It means that Jazz believes Kareshi can only take one small step at a time, and if by staying in the shadows it means every woman in Kareshi has the right to work, she's prepared to do that. We should admire her for that sacrifice.'

'Her *sacrifice*?'

'Kareshi has to be coaxed, not bullied, Tyr. Jazz understands this as I do. Freedom for women to work is the first big step. Freedom for unmarried women to mix openly with men without being shunned by society is the next. Kareshi will take that step, but Jazz is devoted to her people, and I think we can safely trust Jazz to know what's best in this instance.'

'To know what's best for her, or for Kareshi?'

'Don't get so heated, Tyr. For both, of course. And please don't scowl at me like that.'

'You're right, and I apologise.' Britt had done too much for him for him to sound off at her like that. 'I'm still trying to get my head around the feisty girl I knew becoming some sort of reclusive woman.'

'So you didn't shut yourself away from those who loved you?'

Trust Britt to point that out. He forced a smile over his concern for Jazz. 'Point taken.'

'Be happy for her, Tyr. Jazz is a wonderful young woman with the strongest sense of duty where Kareshi is concerned, something I know you can relate to. It makes sense that she doesn't want to cause ripples on the pond.'

'It makes sense to you maybe,' he agreed, 'but Jazz is my friend, and I'm going to see a lot of friends tonight and I'm going to treat them all the same.'

'Then there's nothing to worry about, is there?' Taking his face between her hands, Britt stood on tiptoes to kiss him on both cheeks. 'Now, there are some people outside that door who have waited a long time to give you a big, sloppy welcome without the rest of the world looking on.'

His spirits soared with expectation. 'Eva and Leila are here?'

'With their husbands—I didn't think you'd mind, seeing as Roman and Raffa are your closest friends?'

'I don't mind at all.' He was looking forward to it, and his cynical self reassured him that if he kept it light they wouldn't see anything in his eyes except the happiness a reunion like this would bring.

His middle sister, Eva, was the first into the room, changing the dynamics completely. Eva lived up to her bright red hair with the sharpest tongue this side of a scalpel, and the long space of time since they'd seen each other hadn't dulled Eva's approach. Standing back, she weighed him up. 'You look every bit as formidable as I remember, warrior-boy.'

'I could crush you with one finger, squirt.'

Fists raised, they squared up for a mock fight, and then, bursting into tears, Eva launched herself at him. Pummelling him with her tiny fists, she raged in a shaking voice, 'Don't you ever do that to me again. Do you hear me, Tyr?' Pulling back, she stared at him with furious eyes. 'Don't you *ever* disappear out of my life again without at least having the courtesy to leave me the keys to your muscle car.'

Laughing, he embraced her. 'Promise,' he murmured softly as he kissed the top of her head.

Eyes softened with tears, Eva pulled back to stare at him. 'You've no idea how we've missed you, Tyr.'

'I've missed you too.' How much, they'd never know. 'I can't imagine how I survived all that time without the three of you nagging me.'

As Eva roared with pretended fury, Britt walked to the door and swung it wide. 'Leila!' He was ready to catch his youngest sister and swing her round. Thankfully he stopped in time. 'Wow. You *are* pregnant.'

'Bowling-ball pregnant,' Leila confirmed, laughing and crying all at the same time as they embraced.

'But you look as beautiful as Britt warned me you would.'

Leila huffed a laugh as she stood back. 'If you like waddling hippos, I'm your gal.' She stared at him intently for a moment. 'I can't believe you've come back to us.' His sister's eyes filled with love and concern. 'But life's taken a bite out of you.'

'Enough.' He straightened his jacket. 'We're going to a party, aren't we?'

'We mustn't keep our guests waiting,' Britt agreed, exchanging a look with him as she held the door.

Linking arms with his two younger sisters, he urged them out of the room.

For the first time Jazz could remember, Sharif hadn't shown impatience with her when she wasn't ready to leave for the party at the same time as him and Britt. 'No hurry,' he'd soothed with a smile. 'Just call me when you're ready and I'll come back for you.'

At the time she'd been flapping over what to wear. This might seem like a storm in a teacup to the average bystander, but, when you chose not to socialise in mixed company, it was hard to know what high society in a bustling mining town like Skavanga would expect of a very conservative princess of Kareshi.

'Your smile,' Britt had told Jazz in her usual down-to-earth way, insisting Jazz must show her face on this occasion. 'You don't have to take the traditions of Kareshi to the nth degree when you're staying with us in the frozen north.'

'But if I were photographed—'

'The people of Kareshi could only be proud of their princess. Seeing you with your brother, surrounded by a family who loves you both so much, how could they not be proud of you, Jazz?'

Britt was always hard to argue with, and on that occasion impossible, though Jazz had had to wrestle with her inner demons before she could agree to showing her face in public. Her parents had abused their privilege and neglected their people, leaving Sharif and Jazz in the care of a succession of nannies while their mother had flaunted her beauty on a world stage. Sharif and Jazz had grown up sensitive to the rumblings of discontent in their country, so that when the time came for Sharif to inherit the throne he had moved as quickly as he could to turn the super-tanker round and establish a fair rule so he could make their country safe. Sharif was good and strong and kind and wise, but their troubled childhood in a land of absentee rulers and rampant corruption had left Jazz determined not to cause any more upset, so, however free her spirit, in appearance she was always careful not to offend.

'You should get out of Kareshi more,' Britt had insisted when they had discussed what Jazz would wear for the party. 'It would be good for your people, and good for you.'

Jazz agreed, but Kareshi was steeped in millennia of tradition. Sharif had already given her a job at his racing stables, which had opened the floodgates for every woman in Kareshi to work, should they choose to do so, and Jazz wasn't about to risk their freedom by pushing the traditionalists too far. And it was much easier hiding behind a veil than facing up to a night like this. Staring into the mirror, she wished her heart would stop pounding. Her brother had already left with Britt, so Britt could enjoy a private reunion with her sisters and their long-lost brother, Tyr, at the Skavanga Mining company offices.

Tyr.

Jazz's throat dried. She had always been excited to see the big Viking.

But things were different now, Jazz told herself firmly. She was an adult with responsibilities, not a child who had plagued the life out of her brother's closest friend. She had to guard her feelings.

But Tyr was someone she could always depend on.

Or he had been, until he'd disappeared.

How she'd worried about him—wondered about him—prayed for him to be safe.

And now he was back.

What would he think of her? She was so changed, so solemn and so silent. She wouldn't be playing any tricks on him today.

And she wouldn't be going to the party if she didn't calm down.

Taking a few steadying breaths, she closed her eyes and tried her hardest not to think about Tyr Skavanga. After a few moments, she gave up.

Tyr paused at the entrance to the hotel ballroom and smiled. 'This is beautiful, Britt.'

'No welcome banners,' Eva complained, staring around.

'No. It's all very Britt,' Leila commented approvingly, echoing his own thoughts. 'It's a really classy setting.'

'For a warrior's return,' Eva said proudly, putting her hand on his arm.

'For a homecoming,' he argued gently.

There was no doubt Britt had gone to a lot of trouble. The flowers in the tall vases flanking the easel to one side of the grand double doors were classic and white. The photograph of him Britt had chosen to prop up on the easel showed him laughing and relaxed before he'd entered the theatre of war, where his life had changed completely.

'You look about twenty years older in real life,' Eva informed him helpfully to a chorus of disapproval from their sisters.

'Watch it, shrimp,' he warned playfully, feeling his spirits lift to the point where he thought he might actually enjoy the evening. 'Roman's out of earshot, so you could be heading for a soaking in the chocolate fountain.'

Eva gave a theatrical sigh. 'Death by chocolate suits me.'

'Come on, you two, stop squabbling,' Britt insisted, pulling the big-sister card on both of them.

He walked ahead of his sisters into the lavishly decorated ballroom with its Gothic curlicues and massive, glittering chandeliers, and the first thing he saw when he entered the room was Jazz.

CHAPTER TWO

HOLY CRAP!

Tyr's heart banged in his chest when Jazz turned to look at him. It was as if some invisible electrical cord connected them. What was it he'd said so confidently to Britt only minutes before? *I'm going to see a lot of friends tonight and I'm going to treat them all the same.*

Seriously?

No one else stood a chance of top billing with Princess Jasmina of Kareshi in the room. Britt had been derelict in her description of this new version of the tomboy Jazz, who hadn't just grown up, but who had blossomed like an exotic flower into the most beautiful woman he'd ever seen. Jazz's new air of serenity intrigued him. It was as if she had created a role for herself that she was determined to play out to the full.

He dismissed the new role Jazz had slotted

herself into with a disapproving huff. She was avoiding the truth.

A bit like him, then?

Not a bit like him!

Swiping his hair back, he turned his mind to the flash of fire he'd seen in her eyes when Jazz had first spotted him entering the ballroom. It reminded him of the days when Her Royal Cheekiness had used to goad him on every possible occasion. Level calm had returned to her eyes now that Jazz was concentrating on the group of women surrounding her.

'Tyr?'

He turned to look at Britt.

'She's beautiful, isn't she?'

There was always more to Britt's questions than at first appeared, so he replied with caution. 'I guess.' His world was private. He'd lived alone for too long to share his personal feelings with anyone, even Britt. He should have known his sister didn't need any conversational pointers to read him.

'Don't shake her up, Tyr,' Britt implored. 'Be mild-mannered around her. Don't pull the marauding Viking act. Jazz is trying her hardest to play the conservative card, so that traditionalists aren't rattled when Sharif makes sweeping changes for good in Kareshi.' Britt shook her head for emphasis. 'This evening is really hard for her, Tyr. Being out in mixed company, I mean. But Jazz needs this. She has such a free spirit—but you know that.' Britt frowned. 'She's sacrificed more than we know for Kareshi.'

'Her freedom?' he cut in.

'Tyr, please. Don't make it any harder for her,' Britt begged him with a restraining hand on his arm. 'You, of all people, can surely appreciate the value of sacrifice. So just say hello, be polite and then back off. All right?'

'Thanks for writing the script for me, sis.' He raised an amused brow.

'Just don't mess with Jazz. She's got enough to contend with.'

'I've no intention of messing with Jazz, as you put it, but I'd have to be wood from the neck up not to respond to such a beautiful woman.'

'Just keep your feelings under wraps, Tyr. Spare Jazz the heartache. She's always been half in love with you. And you've been alone a long time, remember.'

'Relax, Britt. I'm not that desperate. I haven't exactly been a saint while I've been away.'

'You can find love in all sorts of unexpected places,' Britt agreed, 'but I don't think Jazz is looking for the type of love you're offering.'

He gave his sister an amused look. 'I hope she isn't looking for love at all.'

'Why, Tyr?' Britt's stare pierced him. 'Would you be jealous?'

'Of Jazz's suitors?' He laughed that off. Offering Britt his arm, he led his sister deeper into the crowded room.

'There are too many alphas in this room,' Britt commented wryly as his sisters' husbands Raffa and Roman waylaid him for a brisk man hug. 'I may drown in testosterone.'

'Don't worry. I'll save you,' Tyr offered as the men broke away to claim their wives.

'That's what I'm afraid of,' Britt murmured.

When they drew closer to Jazz, Britt gave him a warning look and he squeezed her arm to reassure her. 'I remember what you said. I respect Jazz. Always have, always will.'

He didn't hear Britt's reply. The hubbub of excited guests rolled over him like white noise as he kept his gaze fixed on Jazz. Bathed in light beneath a huge chandelier, she was chatting animatedly to an admiring group of women.

'No, Tyr.'

He paused mid-stride with Britt at his elbow.

'Don't you remember what I said? Jazz is going to be heavily chaperoned tonight, and I won't thank you for interfering.'

The corner of his mouth kicked up. 'You still think I'm going to leap on her?'

'I know that look in your eyes. When Jazz marries she's stated her intention to be pure.'

He frowned. 'What are you suggesting?'

'You don't put her in a compromising position. Go easy on her, Tyr. Jazz has barely left Kareshi since the day she was born. Coming to Skavanga is a big adventure for her.'

'I've got no intention of spoiling anything for Jazz. If she has chosen to live her life according to the traditions of Kareshi, then I respect that.'

'Good, because you might be the brother I adore, but if you hurt Jazz—'

'You don't have to say it, Britt.'

'Don't I?' Britt followed his stare straight

ahead to the slim, straight-backed girl wearing the long, concealing robes of Kareshi.

So much for her intention to live a chaste and pure life! Jazz's intentions hadn't changed, but her body was rebelling like you wouldn't believe. Hyper-arousal was an involuntary reaction to a threat, and one glimpse of Tyr Skavanga was all it took to give her all the symptoms. Her muscles were primed for action, while she was tense and ready. Her heart was racing, and her breathing was hectic as adrenalin raced through her system, putting every nerve ending she possessed in super-receptive mode. The flight-or-fight mechanism common to all human beings, whether they were autocratic sheikhs, powerful Scandinavian warriors like Tyr or the highly protected sister of the ruling Sheikh Sharif of Kareshi, could not be controlled by force of will.

But it must be controlled, Jazz determined, glancing at her brother to make sure Sharif had not noticed her response to Tyr.

It wasn't *fear* of Tyr Skavanga raising Jazz's heartbeat as she continued to chat with the group of women surrounding her, but the excitement of rekindling a lifelong friendship with him that was as close to love as it could get. But they weren't children any longer, and Jazz was an unmarried princess of Kareshi, which meant that to love a man outside the family, however innocent that love might be, was absolutely forbidden by the traditionalists in Kareshi. Sharif was a progressive ruler, but Jazz believed that things could only move so fast in a country mired in tradition, and only the fact that tonight was an unmissable family event had ensured her attendance at this party.

She had spent so many years thinking about Tyr, however, that it was impossible to put him out of her mind now he was practically within touching distance. No one knew where Tyr had been for all these years, except perhaps for Sharif, who had been his closest friend since school, and who was as annoyingly silent as the Sphinx on the subject of Tyr Skavanga. They had both attended an elite military college, that much she knew, and then they had both joined Special Forces, where Tyr had been decorated for his courage, but then he'd disappeared. 'Into the desert,' Sharif had told her vaguely. Sharif would never betray a friend's confidence, but had explained that Tyr was working on rebuilding and repairing infrastructure that had been damaged during the years of conflict before Sharif ascended the throne.

Tyr's life experiences had changed him, Jazz realised as she stared at him. There were shadows behind his eyes and deep lines furrowing Tyr's strong face. Whatever her pledge regarding friendships with men outside the family, her heart went out to him.

And bounced when Tyr glanced at her.

It was as if he could feel her interest.

Her cheeks burned as she turned away. Surely Sharif had explained to Tyr that she might be working, and have all the outward appearance of being an independent woman, but she was bound by her duty to Kareshi, and was only marking time until her brother could arrange an advantageous marriage for her—advantageous for Kareshi, that was.

'Skavanga is so glamorous these days, isn't it?'

Thankful to be distracted, she turned to smile at the elderly woman standing next to her. 'This is my first time in Skavanga,' she admitted, 'so

I only know what my brother has told me about a place he's come to love.'

'Before diamonds were discovered in the family mine,' the same woman continued, 'Skavanga was just a tiny mining town beyond the Arctic Circle, scratching a living as best it could, but now our town glitters as brightly as the precious stones your brother mines. We have Sheikh Sharif to thank for playing a major role in the consortium that saved us.'

'You're very kind, but my sister-in-law, Britt, Sharif's wife, has always been the driving force behind the Skavanga mining company.'

The older woman stared at Jazz approvingly as she stood on tiptoe to confide, 'I'm surprised those three powerful men didn't run Britt Skavanga out of town.'

Jazz laughed with all the other women at this reference to the three ambitious men who had formed the consortium that saved the mine. 'I hardly think my brother would run his wife out of town. He adores Britt. And though it's true the consortium provided the funds to mine the diamonds—without Britt?' Jazz shrugged.

'Britt Skavanga has always been a brilliant

businesswoman,' another woman confirmed, smiling at Jazz.

'And now the brand Skavanga Diamonds is an international household name,' the first woman supplied with admiration in her voice.

'How can you all bear to talk business when Tyr Skavanga's home?'

Jazz stared at the pretty young woman who had just spoken up, and couldn't help noticing that the girl was staring at Tyr.

'You must be as excited as I am,' the girl said as she glanced around their group. 'The marriage market has really opened up again. Don't you agree, Princess Jasmina? Have you had chance to speak to Tyr Skavanga yet? I know your brother, His Majesty, and Tyr used to be close friends.'

'They're still friends.' Jazz confirmed this pleasantly, knowing that it shouldn't grate to such an extent to hear Tyr discussed so openly when he was such a private man. Why couldn't she accept the interest of these women and agree with them?

'Is that him over by the door?' another younger woman who had just joined the group demanded.

'How can you mistake him?' the first one exclaimed with affront. 'Tyr Skavanga is easily the best-looking man in this room.'

The latecomer frowned. 'But I thought he was working rough in the desert?'

'I think he might have had a shower since then,' the old lady commented to general amusement.

Jazz couldn't blame the women for being bowled over by Tyr's compelling appearance. Dark and tall, he looked untouchable, yet commanding. Who wouldn't want to know the secrets of a man like that?

'He looks good for someone who's been living like a nomad for so long,' one woman commented.

'Tyr has been working in the desert with the nomadic people,' Jazz felt bound to explain. 'The nomads have a very sophisticated society.'

The same woman feigned a swoon. 'How romantic…billowing Bedouin tents, and long desert nights with a Viking warrior.'

By this time Jazz was tied up in a knot inside. 'Tyr was in the desert building schools and looking for clean water sources.'

When everyone went quiet she could have bitten off her tongue. She hadn't meant to sound preachy and spoil the fun, but to hear people talking about Tyr when they didn't even know him, let alone the valuable work he was doing...

Tyr glanced at her and the world fell away. He would hate to think people were gossiping about him. And she had joined in, Jazz accepted as Tyr's dark stare held hers briefly across the blurring faces of the crowd.

Sharif, who was as sharp as the ceremonial *khanjar*, the curved blade he wore suspended from the jewelled scabbard on his belt, missed nothing, and was instantly at her side. 'Don't you feel well, Jasmina?'

Touching her fingertips to her brow, she used Sharif's reading of the situation to her advantage. 'It is quite noisy, don't you think? Perhaps I won't stay long.'

She wanted to go almost as much as she wanted to stay. She didn't know what she wanted to do.

She should do what was best, which meant staying for as long as politeness dictated and then leaving without drawing attention to herself in any way.

'Just let me know when you're ready to leave, Jasmina,' Sharif said, reading her.

'I will. Thank you.' Gazing up, she touched his sleeve. Beneath his steely exterior Sharif was the kindest and most considerate man she knew.

'And if you're uncomfortable meeting Tyr, just let me know that too.'

'I'm not uncomfortable. We were childhood friends.'

She hated deceiving Sharif, even in her thoughts, and had to take a few deep, steadying breaths. Had she really thought she could handle this?

Sharif's hawk-like gaze flashed from Tyr to her. 'Just so long as you're all right with this, Jasmina?'

'I am. Of course I am.' But her lips felt as stiff as a ventriloquist's doll. She had to face the truth. She couldn't trust her feelings where Tyr Skavanga was concerned.

'Tyr's on his way.'

Sharif's terse warning flashed through her, though she could feel Tyr's approach without needing to turn and look. And then he was in front of them, just inches away.

Jazz remained frozen and stiff as the two men exchanged their customary bunched-fist greeting, then her brother stepped back and she was face-to-face with Tyr Skavanga. For a moment all she could do was study his face and log all the terrible changes, and then she remembered to breathe.

CHAPTER THREE

'HOW WONDERFUL TO see you again, Tyr.'

'And you, Jasmina.'

Wonderful? How inadequate words could be. Her world had been empty and now it was full. The strapping Viking was as fatally compelling as she remembered, but the changes in him were painful to see. Tyr had experienced a lot. Too much, Jazz sensed, and his eyes reflected this. He seemed harder and more cynical, though he was staring down at her with something close to humour in his clear, sharp gaze.

'You've changed, Jazz.'

'So have you.' She said this lightly, but Tyr's essence had changed—frighteningly. The days of teasing him were long gone.

'How are you, Jazz?'

Tyr's sharp gaze pierced her and clearly asked her: *How are you really? Tell me the truth.*

'I'm very well, thank you. And you?'

Her stilted tone brought another flash of amusement to Tyr's dark eyes. 'You look well,' he said.

Heat pooled inside her as he continued to stare down, making a nonsense of her decision to remain aloof from men. And how could she have forgotten the effect of his voice? Tyr's deep, husky tone embraced her like a welcome memory from the past, even as it rang warning bells in her head.

'We must find time to catch up, Jazz.'

She actually gasped at this suggestion. Did Tyr have any idea what he was suggesting? 'Catching up' implied an intimate one-to-one conversation, which was absolutely forbidden. Private time with a man apart from her brother, Sharif, could never happen, but as Sharif was called away to greet some of their other guests she found herself alone with Tyr. Jazz's cheeks flamed red with embarrassment. The connection between them hadn't been lost. If anything, the passage of time had only made it stronger.

Britt saved her. Having organised the event, Britt was easily the busiest woman in the room, but still she had spotted Jazz, who was marooned on her own personal desert island with Tyr, and quickly came across to offer a life raft.

'Jazz, there are some people I think you'd like to meet. Excuse us, please, Tyr.' Smiling briefly at her brother, she whisked Jazz away.

Jazz exhaled shakily as they crossed the ballroom. 'Thank you for rescuing me.'

'From those two dinosaurs?' Britt laughed. 'I could see Sharif's tension a mile off, and when Tyr came over to speak to you I knew it was time to launch a rescue mission.'

Jazz glanced round to find Tyr was still watching her.

'Come on.' Britt squeezed her arm. 'There are lots of great people for you to meet.'

Jazz counted herself lucky to have a sister-in-law like Britt on her side. Britt acted as a sounding board, and, with no other female relatives to confide in, it was reassuring to know she could always talk to Britt. Jazz really valued her growing friendship with the three Skavanga sisters, though doubted they understood her point of view where her chosen lifestyle was concerned, as they came from such a different world.

'I'm going to introduce you to a really nice

crowd,' Britt promised, linking arms with Jazz. 'We'll leave the men to brood.'

Jazz blushed. She could feel Tyr's stare on her back, halfway across the room.

'Are you all right?' Britt whispered discreetly during a lull in the conversation with the crowd they'd joined. 'I saw the way you looked at Tyr.'

Britt's eyes were full of compassion. Had everyone noticed? 'I'm fine.' She smiled to reassure Britt. 'I can handle Tyr.'

Britt smiled back, but nothing about that smile convinced Jazz that Britt believed her as they both glanced around at Tyr. 'He cares about you, Jazz. We all do.'

Impulsively, Jazz gave Britt a hug. Britt was the closest thing she had to a sister, but, however much she thought of Britt, nothing could derail Jazz's determination to live a life beyond reproach in service to her country.

Jazz Kareshi was all grown up. Tyr's mouth tugged fractionally at the irony of doing everything in his power to avoid finding his best friend's sister attractive and failing miserably. Jazz had grown into a beautiful woman and he could look at nothing else. He should be grateful to Britt for whisking Jazz away before his interest became more obvious. The fact that Sharif had stood between him and Jazz until Sharif was called away had irritated the hell out of him. He'd known Jazz since she wore pigtails and braces; couldn't they even talk to each other now? They were both powerful men, and used to having their own way, but it seemed there were some things Sharif would like to deny Tyr, like catch-up time with Jazz.

'Jazz seems happy tonight,' he commented when Sharif joined him, determined to find out everything there was to know about Jazz.

'My sister is always happy. Why would she not be?'

'No reason, Sharif.' He returned Sharif's suspicious glance with a level stare. 'Are you trying to keep her away from me? Relax,' he said as Sharif stiffened with affront. 'Jazz is your sister and I respect that. I wouldn't do anything to cause either of you embarrassment.'

'Jasmina has chosen to distance herself from the modern world for her own reasons, not because anyone, least of all me, has tried to confine her.'

He stared into the eyes of a man he'd known and trusted most of his life, and knew instantly that Sharif was telling him the truth.

'Jasmina believes that while I implement change for the better, she must reassure the more conservative groups in our country by remaining a very traditional princess. We will both do anything we can to avoid the chaos of our parents' rule.'

'I understand that, and I respect it,' Tyr assured his friend, following Sharif's stare across the room to where Jazz was standing. Both Sharif and Jazz were determined to do everything they could for their people, even if that meant sacrificing their own happiness.

'Jasmina is finding the party a little overwhelming, I think,' Sharif remarked as if reading his mind.

'It must be a conflict for her—coming out into mixed company, I mean.'

They shared a smile as he remembered the tomboy who had been at the forefront of every adventure, while Sharif had always had to consider his dignity and look forward to what was best for Kareshi.

'And you, Tyr?' Sharif looked at him with concern. 'How are you enjoying the party?'

'Like Jazz. Mixing with so many people at once is something of an ordeal.' His lips pressed down at this rueful admission, but both he and Jazz had chosen the solitary life, if for very different reasons. 'But I'm grateful to Britt for arranging this party. Britt is right—I need to be back amongst people I love.'

This was true, but there were too many people here and far too much noise. Five minutes alone with Jazz, someone he didn't have to explain every little thing to because they had that long history of friendship behind them, would have been more than enough for him, but he couldn't share that opinion with Sharif.

'Tyr—'

'Over here—'

Another friend. Another photograph.

He should be more gracious. He would try, but the flare of candlelight on crystal was like a barrage of spotlights directed on his face. Everyone wanted to know where he'd been, what he'd done, what he'd seen. Only Jazz shone like a beacon in the midst of all the uproar. She was an oasis in the desert of his life, and his gaze sought her out hungrily.

'I'm guessing you'd rather be back in the desert, Tyr?'

Jolted out of his reverie, he turned to lock stares with Sharif. 'You guessed right.'

It was the silence of the desert that had first imprinted itself on his heart, and Sharif and Jazz were an integral part of the land he loved. He loved their harsh country and the hostile terrain. He loved them. The hardship of his work in the desert soothed him. It distracted him from other things, ugly things in his past. Up to tonight he'd had no wish to rekindle gentle feelings that seemed to have died inside him, but now?

'I wish you the very best of evenings, Tyr.'

He refocused on Sharif.

'But stay away from my sister.'

It took him a moment to realise that he'd been staring at Jazz the whole time they'd been talking.

'Don't make Jazz's life even harder than she makes it for herself, Tyr.'

'I wouldn't do anything to hurt either of you,' he assured his friend.

As he spoke, a group of guests chose that moment to draw Sharif away, leaving Tyr free to gaze at Jazz uninterrupted. Strange to think the happy, carefree girl he remembered would never be truly free again and that the best thing he could do for Jazz was to butt out of her life altogether.

He tried to ignore her. He chatted to some guests, but while Jazz was in the same room as him he couldn't concentrate. Were they supposed to ignore each other for the rest of the night? He was so tense that his expression was fierce as he whirled around when someone touched his arm. He was shocked to see an old lady staring up at him. 'I'm so sorry.' His expression softened instantly. 'Please forgive me.'

'There's no need to apologise,' she said with a smile. 'I just wanted to tell you how good it is to see the Skavanga family reunited. And I think it's especially significant to see Sheikh Sharif's sister here. I understand why Princess Jasmina has chosen to live her life the way she has. I was talking to her earlier. It must have been a big step for her to take, and an even bigger one for her to be here tonight. She's obviously courageous. And what a beautiful girl she is. She is so lucky to have a brother who clearly adores her.'

Tyr made polite noises as the charming old lady chatted on, but what he really appreciated was the excuse to stare openly at Jazz. He'd been a prisoner of war for a time, and understood that captivity could be as much a condition of the mind as the body, and his heart went out to Jazz. He would not exchange one moment of his life now for Jazz's confined existence, but he couldn't blame her for her choices when Jazz was as much a servant to duty as he.

As if sensing his interest, Jazz turned to look at him, and for the briefest moment her expression held all the warmth and mischief of the past.

'Well, I mustn't take up all your time.'

Realising he'd been ignoring the old lady, he quickly turned to her. 'You must once more forgive me. I was distracted.'

'By Princess Jasmina?' The old lady smiled up at him. 'I'm not surprised.'

He shrugged with amusement at being caught out. These were good people, all keen to welcome him back, and he should show them more respect. He would. Tonight would go smoothly from now on, if he just could stick to one simple rule: Jazz Kareshi was off-limits.

But within moments a group had formed around him and all they wanted to talk about were his exotic friends from Kareshi. One of the women pointed to Sharif, who even Tyr had to admit looked striking in his flowing robes.

'The sheikh is exactly what I think of when I imagine a desert warrior,' she enthused. 'Tell me, Tyr,' she added with a smile, 'did they hand out handsome pills at your school?'

'No. Cold showers and the birch,' he murmured distractedly, wondering what the crowd of young women around Jazz could have said to make her face light up. Leaving the women around him still exclaiming with outrage on his behalf at his comments about his old school, he made his way towards her. There was only one woman in this room who held his attention and only one woman in the world who could provoke any sort of response in him. He'd clamped down on feelings in order to survive, and had thought he'd lost the knack of feeling anything, until tonight.

Britt was in the same group as Jazz, and smiled as he walked up to them. Sharif's hooded stare followed him across the crowded room. He glanced back to reassure his friend, and to tell him at the same time that they might be as close as brothers, but no one told Tyr how to live his life. But could he risk infecting a bright spirit like Jazz with his darkness? Hadn't Jazz heaped enough pain on herself without him interfering? Freedom was a gift he had always taken for granted, but Jazz was a glaring example that life wasn't always so straightforward. Jazz's boundaries hadn't expanded. When she grew up they had shrunk.

There was another quick look from Jazz that took him right back to the tricks they used to play on each other when they were younger: burrs beneath the saddle, itching powder in their riding boots. Innocent times before the shadows crept in. He'd have a short, polite conversation with her and then move on, he decided. What could be more innocent than that? He'd ask her about the riding stables. Britt had told him how much Jazz enjoyed working there. He wouldn't make a single comment about the remote racing stable being yet another way for Jazz to shut herself off from the world. And he certainly wouldn't tell her about the arousal that lanced through him each time their glances met and held. They were good friends. They would remain good friends. They had always been able to ease their way back into an easy friendship, even after months apart.

That was then and this is now, and now everything has changed.

True, the past could not be recaptured, and the future was not his to command, but seizing the moment was his particular skill and this chance to talk to Jazz was up for grabs.

CHAPTER FOUR

JUST AS TYR came within earshot, Britt whisked Jazz away, explaining that she had arranged the place cards on their table so that Jazz wouldn't have to sit anywhere near Tyr, or any other single man. As Britt smiled reassurance into her eyes, Jazz was reminded again how much she valued their friendship.

'I'm so glad you're here to share Tyr's homecoming. It wouldn't have been the same without you, Jazz.'

'I'm sorry if I seem tense to you.'

'You feel awkward around men?' Britt shrugged. 'That's hardly surprising. You should get out of Kareshi more. I'm going to speak to your brother about it.'

'Please don't give Sharif anything more to worry about. I'm happy in Kareshi. You know how much I love my work, and—'

'And how you live under your own self-imposed guard while you're there? Yes. I know all about that, Jazz—only allowing yourself this briefest of trips outside the country?'

'I know you find the way I live hard to understand, but please believe me, Britt. This is the right thing to do for my country.'

Britt shook her head. 'Locking yourself away can never be the right thing to do. It would benefit your people *and* you if you travelled more.'

'I can never forget that I'm a princess of Kareshi,' Jazz argued, trying her hardest not to glance at Tyr. 'Or that with that title comes duty and responsibility.'

'But not a ball and chain, surely?'

Britt's expression made Jazz laugh. 'Now you're exaggerating. Anyone would think I was my own jailer.'

'But aren't you?' Britt turned serious. 'Beware of squashing your spirit completely, Jazz. Don't turn yourself into something you're not.'

Jazz's eyes sparkled. 'Like an embittered old shrew, do you mean?'

'There's no chance of that.' Britt laughed. 'And now we've got my brother to contend with.' With a sigh she stood aside as the crowds parted to allow the handsome Viking through.

'Don't look so worried. I can handle Tyr.'

Jazz could only hope her heart was listening.

Tyr paused for a moment to check Sharif was still talking to the ambassador and his wife, before approaching the family table for dinner. He didn't want to cause Jazz a moment's discomfort, but, as if sensing his approach, Sharif called his sister over.

Britt walked over. 'You're looking thoughtful, Tyr.'

'I am thoughtful.'

'But you'll stay and see the evening through?'

'Of course I will. I appreciate everything you've done for me.'

'But you would have preferred something a little more low-key.'

'No, in this you're right,' he admitted. 'Better to see everyone at once.'

Britt cocked her head. 'Get it over with?'

He looked at his sister with amusement. 'I couldn't possibly comment.'

And then the ever-changing pattern of friends

reshaped again, leaving Jazz all alone in a halo of light.

Jazz made her way to the family table, only to find Tyr there ahead of her. Relaxing back on one of the gilt chairs, he was surveying the party with his cool dark gaze. She was about to turn around, to go and find Britt, or her brother, but Tyr was already on his feet, holding out a chair. 'Jazz.'

No man should smile at her like that—so openly—so invitingly.

There was a belief in Kareshi that members of the opposite sex could never stare directly into each other's eyes without there being some form of sexual implication.

'Tyr.' Had she always felt so awkward around him?

She knew the answer to that question. They had never been awkward with each other in the past, but a new tension had entered their relationship and that seemed set to stay. Neither of them was the same person they'd been ten years ago. Britt was right in saying a lot of water had passed under the bridge since then.

It was only when she sat down that Jazz realised Tyr had ignored Britt's carefully arranged place cards completely. Britt had assured her she wasn't going to be sitting anywhere near Tyr, so he must have moved the cards around.

So what was she going to do about it? Make some excuse and move halfway round the table? Wouldn't that seem rude? Wouldn't that be ridiculous, considering they were the only people at the table? Her heart thundered as Tyr's mouth slanted in a smile.

'So, what have you been doing with yourself while I've been away, Jazz?'

She stared into a pair of eyes that had always been able to devastate her nervous system. 'Where to start?' She gave a shaky laugh.

'Jazz?'

Tyr's voice sounded as if it were coming to her from a long way away, down an echoing tunnel. She should not be here. She should not be talking to a man. And this was not just any man, but Tyr Skavanga, a man who demanded every woman's attention, especially Jazz's, and to the point where, having stared into his eyes, she couldn't look away. 'It's been a long time, Tyr.'

Tyr's mouth curved with wry amusement at

this comment. And no wonder, when that was probably the lamest thing she could have said. They'd been friends for years and she couldn't think of a single question to ask him? Not even when she was so hungry to know every detail of Tyr's missing life.

Sharing none of her reserve, Tyr continued to study her face as if he would like to record every tiny detail. This made her deeply uncomfortable, though thankfully, Britt was heading towards them at speed. And then out of the blue her courage returned, and, holding Tyr's gaze, she accepted the connection, as she told him with her eyes that things could never be the same between them again, and that he mustn't tease her and flirt with her as if she were still ten years old.

'Tyr?' Britt's voice sounded brittle as she hovered over them. 'Have you changed my place cards around?'

'Would I?' Resting back in his chair, Tyr cast a lazy glance up at his sister, which made Britt huff impatiently, but it was too late for Britt to change them round again as some important guests had arrived and were waiting to be seated.

Neither Sharif nor Tyr could ever be said to have forgotten their manners. They were both round the table in an instant, holding chairs out for their visitors. Sharif even put a restraining hand on Britt's arm when she would have changed places with Jazz. 'The ambassador,' he murmured discreetly.

Damned by etiquette, Jazz thought as Tyr sat down at her side. The ambassador and his wife were Britt's guests of honour tonight, and as Britt and Sharif were hosting the party it was unthinkable that the ambassador would sit next to anyone but Britt.

When everyone was seated and chatting happily, Britt managed a discreet word while Tyr was talking to the ambassador. 'Are you sure you're all right sitting here next to Tyr, Jazz?'

Smiling, Jazz confirmed, 'Of course I am.'

What else could she say?

Was she the only one to feel the tension building around the table? Jazz wondered. She was doing everything she could to ignore Tyr, but he was sitting so close, her whole body was tingling with awareness. How could she remain insensible to his heat, or to the compelling presence of the big Viking at her side? She had forbidden herself every sensual delight reality could offer, and exploring the forbidden in her mind had become a favourite pastime. But not tonight. She must not allow her thoughts to wander tonight. Gathering her robe a little closer, she forced the direction of her thoughts away from the devastating man at her side.

For around five seconds.

'Would you like some water, Jazz?'

Staring into Tyr's eyes made her heart race. 'Yes, please.' She sounded so formal and distant. Which was good, she reminded herself, even if it was directly opposed to what was happening inside her.

'Will you be staying in Skavanga long, Princess Jasmina?'

She turned with relief to the woman sitting on her other side, but even that didn't help, because her mind had taken a photograph of Tyr that meant she could chat intelligently enough, while studying every detail of Tyr in her mind. His hair was thick and tawny, and sun-bleached around his face where it hung in rebel tousles no matter how many times he swept it back. His stubble was sharp and black, and thick, though he must have shaved before he came to the party…and she could smell his cologne. Everything about him spelled danger. Everything about Tyr Skavanga was what she had vowed to avoid. He was wearing black on black tonight, when every other man at the table, apart from Sharif in his ceremonial robes, was dressed in a conventional dinner suit, with a conventional shirt and a conventional tie. Tyr had always bucked the trend, she remembered.

'More water, Princess?' Tyr's gravelly voice shook her round. 'Or something else, perhaps?'

'No, thank you.' How prim she sounded. But those wicked eyes— How dared he look at her like that? Storm-grey and darkening, Tyr's eyes were lit with a disturbing understanding of her inner turmoil. He had always been able to read her mind. It was a skill that had made her mad when she was younger, and which now made her uncomfortably aware. And that firm mouth that she had all too often imagined kissing her.

She must forget that now.

She must!

'Are you sure? No more water?' he prompted.

Her cheeks flamed red. 'Yes, I'm sure.' Frowning, she looked at him with what Jazz realised was the type of black look she would have given him when they were both younger, which was far too intimate a reminder of how close they'd once been.

'Your napkin, Jazz?'

She dragged in a sharp breath as Tyr leaned towards her. Shaking out her napkin, he moved to lay it on her lap. His face was so close to hers, her cheeks were burning. The brush of starched linen against her skin sent shivers of arousal streaking through her. The whisper of its touch against her thigh shocked her to think that she could be so easily seduced. Tyr was a force of nature, Jazz reassured herself. Anyone would feel as she did. She should leave now and have nothing more to do with him.

'You look beautiful tonight, Jazz.'

You can't say that!

But how she wanted to hear it.

Tyr's eyes were warm and amused when she didn't reply. Didn't he know how dangerous this was? Didn't he care?

Eva saved the day, taking control of the conversation around the table. Smiling at her brother proudly, Eva proceeded to tell everyone that Tyr had been born with a map and compass in his hand, and when everyone laughed, Jazz was able to relax as the spotlight swung away from her.

But not for long.

'How do you feel about wanderlust, Jazz?'

Why did Tyr have to ask her that question? Why did he have to speak to her at all? She stared into his eyes. This was her opportunity to make her position clear to him. 'I've always believed there's no place like home, and so far I've had no reason to change my mind.' Unless a marriage organised by Sharif took her to a new country, and a new family, where Jazz had no doubt she would be treasured like one of the hard, blue-white diamonds her brother and Tyr mined. She experienced a chill of apprehension at that thought. And then with everything inside her warning her to leave it, she turned back to Tyr. 'I have never felt your desire to keep moving and searching.'

'Maybe because you've never given yourself

that chance,' Tyr cut in, resting his chin on his hand as he stared at her with amusement.

'Tyr's dangerous to know and even more dangerous to love,' Eva confided across the table, laughing as everyone else laughed with her.

Jazz laughed too, thankful to Eva for diluting the tension with a joke. Joining in with the laughter seemed safest, and she thanked her lucky stars she would never be in a position to find out just how dangerous Tyr Skavanga could be.

'We never know when Tyr's going to disappear again,' Eva continued, capturing everyone's attention again. 'He might not be there if I blink.'

More laughter followed this, but Jazz felt a pang of loss as if Tyr had already left them.

'Don't worry. I'm sticking around,' he confided, but why couldn't he say that to the whole table, instead of just to her?

He pretty much kept his promise to leave Jazz alone right up to the moment when Britt mounted the rostrum to deliver her speech of welcome and the lights dimmed. This left Britt alone in the spotlight and the rest of the room in shadow. Sharif had turned his chair around to listen to his wife, encouraging everyone else at the table to do the same.

'What?' Jazz murmured when she felt his interest switch to her. 'Will you please stop staring at me, Tyr?'

'No.'

Jazz's voice was a fierce whisper, his was a lazy drawl, and her little growl of anger could have come straight from the old days, and that made him smile. Then she must have decided that if he was going to provoke her, she was going to lob back some polite and wholly innocuous conversation, and as he continued to study Jazz at his leisure, he was so engrossed he barely heard her question.

When he'd computed it, he frowned. 'Did I manage to bring water to that village?' he repeated. 'Yes, I did. How do you know about that?'

'Don't worry. Sharif didn't betray you. I happened to see the invoice for aqua-cleaning machinery come in, and I knew Sharif didn't have any current projects running, so I put two and two together.'

'And came up with me?'

'I do have some original thoughts that aren't stamped approved by my brother.'

'I'm sure you do. And was that a hint of amusement in your voice I detected, Princess?'

She raised a brow. 'Am I so dull?'

He paused. 'You've changed.'

'Don't mock me, Tyr. I'm not sixteen any longer.'

'This I can see for myself.'

'Then you shouldn't be looking.'

They were silent for some time after that.

The speeches ended and the prizes had all been handed out. The lights went up and Britt returned to their table to be congratulated by Sharif. His friend was a different character when he was with Britt, Tyr noted. Britt was a soothing hand on the warrior brow—something Tyr badly needed.

Anything that could distract him from his feelings for Jazz—feelings that clawed at his senses—would be good.

'You're like a seething volcano of pent-up energy,' Eva commented, picking up on his tension. 'Thor minus the hammer, unless you're keeping that under the table?'

He hummed with amusement as he settled back. Eva knew him too well. She could sense his hunting instinct. He was the wolf. Jazz was the petal in danger of being trampled underfoot. Watching Britt persuade Sharif to dance, he felt his hunting instinct sharpen as one by one the other couples at the table joined them, leaving just one elderly man and woman to chaperone him and Jazz. And as the elderly couple were currently engrossed in their own conversation…

'So, Princess Jasmina.'

Taking a deep breath, Jazz turned to stare at him. 'Can the Sunday title, Tyr. You don't need to pretend with me. You've called me Jazz from the first time we met, and I'm still Jazz to you.'

Mentally, he reeled back with surprise, then rebuked himself for forgetting that Jazz might have changed outwardly, but inwardly she was the same girl. He searched her eyes, but she turned away, then tensed when a group passed by and bowed to her in respect for her rank. 'You can't blame people,' he pointed out as Jazz chewed her lip unhappily. 'You're not the tomboy to them you always were to me. You're a princess.'

'But that's just it, Tyr. I can't buy into the title when I haven't done anything to deserve it.'

'But you will,' he said confidently, relieved that at least they were talking.

'Perhaps you're right,' Jazz admitted with a sigh. 'But I don't feel any different from anyone else. Except…'

'Except?' he prompted, angling his chin to stare into her eyes.

'Except I think you should bow to me.'

She said this with all the old humour and, sitting back, Tyr laughed with relief to think the girl he used to know was still in there somewhere. 'Now, why should I bow to you, Princess?'

'Viking warlords need to be put in their place by a princess of the desert.'

'And what place is that?'

Jazz's cheeks flushed attractively with heat. 'A dungeon, preferably,' she said as if realising that this conversation had already gone too far.

'But I didn't think you were frightened of anything?'

She fixed him with an unwavering gaze. 'You're right. I'm not.'

'So if there's any little service I can offer you, at that time and that time only, I will be sure to bow.'

For once in his life he broke eye contact first. If any other woman had looked at him the way Jazz had so briefly looked at him, he would have anticipated a very different outcome to this evening. High time for a reminder that when it came to the mating game, Jazz was so innocent she didn't know the rules.

But he couldn't ignore her for long. 'You look good, Jazz. Life is obviously treating you well.'

'Very well, thank you,' she said primly. 'You look good too.'

He huffed with amusement. 'There's no need for you to be polite with me.'

As Jazz's eyes clouded with concern, he warned, 'Don't get into it. This is a party, remember?'

'A party in your honour, Tyr, so I'm afraid you have to accept that people care about you. I don't suppose anyone knows how to behave around you when you've been away for so long.'

He sat back. He liked this new Jazz. She was as much of a challenge beneath that prim exterior as she had ever been, but he liked the wild child from the past better. This new version of Jazz was a tightly strung instrument that only played to Jazz's self-imposed restrictive tune.

'It might help if you talked about things that matter to you, Tyr, like the ideals you were fighting for.'

'Like what?' He tensed. She had hit a nerve. It was Jazz that had the problem, not him.

'Like freedom, Tyr,' Jazz said calmly.

'Freedom?' He laughed incredulously as he stared at her. 'And what do you know about that?'

'What do you mean?' she protested. 'I'm free.'

'Are you, Jazz?'

She couldn't meet his eyes, and then she whispered, 'You always represented freedom to me, Tyr.'

'I did?' An invisible hand grabbed his heart. Years of feeling nothing had hit the buffers tonight, he realised, and all thanks to Jazz Kareshi.

'You've always done what you wanted, Tyr,' she explained. 'You could go where you wanted, do what you wanted to do, when you wanted to.'

'You can too,' he insisted, staring hard into Jazz's eyes. 'This is the twenty-first century.'

'Not in Kareshi.' Jazz smiled. 'And we should stop talking like this before someone takes a photograph of us having this conversation.'

'Britt wouldn't allow the paparazzi within a hundred miles of here,' he reassured her as Jazz flashed an anxious gaze around.

'Please don't tease me, Tyr.' There was real concern in her voice. 'You've got no idea what it's like for Sharif in Kareshi. He's doing everything he can to help our people, but a strident minority still continues to rail against progress. I'm doing all I can to reassure that section of our society.'

'Public opinion will do that,' he argued. 'Sacrificing yourself will hardly be noticed in the grand scheme of things, but your life will have been ruined—and all by you.'

'And if I want to do this?'

When he remained silent, Jazz shook her head. 'I should have known you wouldn't understand. You're too like Sharif. He says I'm going too far.'

'Well, aren't you?' he cut in.

'The two of you are as close as brothers,' Jazz

said, ignoring his comment. 'You can both do as you like, when you like, and you take that right for granted, but life isn't like that for me, Tyr. I'm a royal princess of Kareshi and I have a duty to uphold certain standards.'

'And what does that entail?' His heart was sinking even as he asked the question, because he knew Jazz's answer would involve more sacrifice, more confinement, more restrictions. Basically a smaller life for Jazz, and, knowing her as he did, that felt like a tragic waste of life to him.

'I'll just have to see what the future holds,' she said. 'Sharif has been approached by the Emir of Qadar.'

He had no idea what that meant, but it didn't sound good.

'It would be a great match for me, Tyr. Our two countries share a boundary.'

'A *match*?' He looked at her disbelievingly. 'As in marriage?'

Jazz blushed. 'This is only the start of negotiations.'

He raised a brow. 'So you're a bargaining counter now?'

'Of course not. Sharif would never marry me off to someone I couldn't get along with.'

'Get along with?' He spat out the words like something nasty in his mouth. 'Aren't you supposed to love the person you marry?'

'Love?' Briefly, Jazz seemed bewildered by the concept. 'I don't even know him.'

'Do you think this is wise?'

'I've *seen* him.'

'You've seen him?' he repeated. 'Oh, well, that's all right, then.'

'Don't mock me, Tyr. This is our way in Kareshi.'

'Freedom to love should be everyone's way in every country of the world.'

'But Sharif has already broken with tradition by allowing me to pursue a career, and sometimes you have to be content. I agree that by staying in Kareshi I could achieve a lot, but if by marrying the emir I can take some of the burden off Sharif's shoulders—'

'Sharif's a grown man,' he cut in, having heard enough. 'Sharif is a proven ruler. What about *your* life, Jazz? What about *you*?'

'Me?'

He didn't know which of them was surprised more by his passionate outburst.

'Kareshi is my life,' Jazz insisted. 'Anything I can do to help my country I'll do gladly.'

'You're repeating yourself, Jazz,' he said. 'And if you really want to help your country, why not stay in Kareshi and work?'

'But the emir… I agreed Sharif could meet with him.'

'And you can stop him doing that in a few words.' He fixed Jazz with a stare, which she avoided.

Heaving a sigh, she glanced around, presumably to see if anyone had noticed this heated discussion. 'I don't want to stop him,' she admitted, leaning close. 'If my marriage to the emir will benefit Kareshi, then that's good enough for me.'

'What you've just suggested is outrageous.' He sat back. Subject closed.

'Fine words, Tyr, but you weren't born into the royal family of Kareshi. You're free to do anything you want and I'm not. It's that simple.'

'Nothing is ever that simple.' As he should know.

Grinding his jaw with frustration, he had to remind himself that this was a party, and that it was better for them both to calm down. At least for now.

CHAPTER FIVE

THERE WAS NO more chance to speak as Britt and Sharif had returned to sit at the table. In spite of his lifelong friendship with Sharif, he couldn't believe his friend was going along with Jazz's crazy idea, or that neither of them could talk Jazz out of the narrow path she had chosen to follow.

'Stop seething, Tyr.'

The sound of Jazz's voice, low and urgent, made him turn to look at her.

'You're making me uncomfortable,' she explained in an undertone, 'and people will notice.'

'You're making me uncomfortable with all this talk of an arranged marriage to a man you don't even know,' he countered. 'What makes you think you've changed that much, Jazz? When you were younger you would have laughed an idea like that out of court.'

'Exactly. We're both older now, and I'm in a

position to do something to help my country by making at least one of our borders secure.'

Shaking his head to shut her up, he hit Jazz with a cynical look.

'Allying our two countries will be good for Kareshi,' she insisted.

'But Kareshi is rich, since Sharif took over, and your brother is a wise ruler. Why the hell would he agree to sacrificing his sister for nothing more than political expediency?'

'If he thinks it makes me happy—'

'Ha! I can't believe Sharif goes along with that.'

'Tyr, please keep your voice down.'

'Whatever you say, Princess, but I don't think you've thought this through.'

'I'm not going to argue with you. I'm saying this is how it's going to be.'

'What happened to the girl I used to know?'

Jazz threw him an accusatory look, but there was something in her eyes that suggested deep down she agreed with him. It was sad to think her stubbornness wouldn't allow Jazz to admit she was wrong so she could put a stop to these crazy marriage plans.

Sensing something was going on between them, Sharif glanced round. Tyr exchanged a brief look with his friend, lips pressed down to express regret at the fact that this was one time when he couldn't help Sharif out. Sharif shrugged. Jazz had always been stubborn. Once she got an idea into her head, they both knew she ran with it until Jazz, or the concept, ran out of steam.

After feeling nothing for so long, Tyr felt this urge to help Jazz overwhelming him. He would like to get very close indeed to Jazz Kareshi.

All the more reason to sit back and ignore her.

This was turning into one hell of an evening.

And it was about to get worse.

As he released a sigh of frustration, Jazz looked at him with something in her eyes that made his senses go into free fall. 'Don't play games with me, Jazz,' he mouthed in an undertone.

'I'm not playing games with you.'

So her eyes were playing games with him—her lips too. And flushed cheeks betrayed her more than any excuses she could give. The laws of attraction took no prisoners. Nor did they show concern for a self-contained warrior who'd had his armour split wide open tonight, or a conservative princess who had just rediscovered her wings.

'Tyr.'

He glanced up with relief to see his sister Britt. Putting one hand on the back of his chair and the other on the back of Jazz's chair, his sister bound them briefly. 'How are you two enjoying the evening so far?'

You two? Should he tell her the truth and ruin Britt's evening after all her hard work on his behalf? He was tense beyond belief, and Jazz was—Jazz. 'I'm having a wonderful time. It's been a great chance to catch up.'

'Do you mean that?' Jazz murmured when his sister had left them to rejoin Sharif.

'I've learned a lot.' Like Jazz's freedom shouldn't depend on some misguided idea of how she could best help her country.

'Why are you staring at me like that, Tyr?'

'Am I staring at you?' He guessed Jazz would have to be contained in a hermetically sealed suit for him not to stare. In a traditional, slim-fitting ankle-length gown in a rich shade of midnight-blue, edged with subtle bronze thread, she was dressed perfectly to suit her character; that was to say, demure with a touch of fire. He'd like to see that spark inside her ignite. What would it take? he wondered. With her waist-length inky-black hair covered with a filmy veil, she looked stunning.

'Tyr,' she warned, staring down at her hands, 'will you please stop staring at me?'

'You can't blame me for looking at the most interesting thing in the room.'

'But I do blame you. I'm not a child, any longer. You can't tease and flirt with me as you used to do.' Jazz shook her head, making her filmy veil shiver. 'Don't you understand anything? Or are you intent on making my life more difficult?'

'That's the last thing I want, Princess, but it is usual to hold a conversation with the person sitting next to you at the dinner table.'

'You're impossible.'

Jazz whipped her head away so fast her veil slipped back. Before she could rearrange it, the soft nape of her neck was revealed as her hair swung to one side. The wave of disappointment that hit him when she quickly pulled the veil forward and that delicate sliver of naked flesh disappeared was a real eye-opener. He really did have it bad. And then Jazz proved his suspicion that the grit was still there when she stood to propose a toast. Raising her glass of juice, she turned to face Britt.

'I would like to propose a toast of thanks to a wonderful woman and a dear friend: my brother's wife, Britt. I want to thank you on behalf of everyone here for the work you've put in to make tonight such a wonderful success. I couldn't love you more if you were my own sister.' Emotion made Jazz pause for a moment as murmurs of approval rose around her. 'The charity we're supporting tonight means a lot to all of us seated round this table, and tonight is also an opportunity for us to welcome Tyr home.'

Tyr tensed as Jazz stared straight at him. This evening would be over soon, but something told him the repercussions from tonight would spread out like ripples on a pond and touch them all.

Even after a few days, it still felt strange being at home with his sisters after so long away. All four of them together at one time like this was practically unique, but Britt, Eva and Leila had put their husbands out to graze for the day so they could spend time with him—and with Jazz. At least, that was what they'd told him, but for the past half-hour they'd cut him out and talked exclusively to Jazz. And in ever-diminishing whispers that left him super-alert and ultra-suspicious.

'You're not supposed to be listening,' Eva complained when he glanced up. 'Get back to watching sport.'

Yes. He was the token man, allowed to remain in the same room as his sisters and Jazz, providing he took the lid off the nuts and poured the sodas for them. With his feet crossed on the coffee table and a bottle of beer in his hand, he'd been invisible up to this point.

'Could you speak up?' he requested dryly. 'I'm having trouble hearing you.'

'If you must know,' Eva fired at him from her position at the head of the table, 'Jazz is in a fix.'

'A fix? What does that mean?' He swung round to stare at Jazz.

'It's nothing.' Jazz tried to brush this off with an airy sweep of her hand.

'You've started, so you might as well finish,'

he observed dryly, noting her cheeks had turned bright red.

'If you must know,' Eva cut in, 'Jazz has today received a formal offer from the Emir of Qadar.'

He groaned inwardly. Time had run out. In the interest of learning more, he acted dumb. 'What kind of offer?'

'Oh, for goodness' sake,' Eva exclaimed, glancing round the table. 'I know you're a man, but you must have some idea?'

He shrugged. 'I'm sure you'll enlighten me.'

Clicking her tongue against the roof of her mouth, Eva—as he had hoped she would—hurried to fill in the details. 'An offer of marriage, dummkopf. And soon.'

Soon? He didn't want to hear another word. He knew his face must be as black as thunder as he appeared to consider this bombshell.

'The Emir of Qadar?' he said at last, lips pressing down as he nodded his head, acting impressed. 'Big country. Important title. That's quite a compliment for Jazz, isn't it?'

Britt put a restraining hand on Eva's arm when she sucked in a breath.

'Well, isn't it?' he said mildly.

Eva scowled, while Leila bit her lip, and Britt looked troubled. Jazz avoided his stare altogether.

'Is anyone going to explain?' he requested mildly, seething inside.

Eva took the bait. 'May I?' she said, looking at Jazz with concern.

Jazz shrugged and appeared resigned. 'Go right ahead. It will soon be public knowledge, so, why not?'

Taking a deep breath, Eva stared into his eyes. She was sending him a strong message of sympathy for Jazz, along with an entreaty for him to do something the heck about it. 'You might not think it such a compliment when I tell you that the emir has insisted on Jazz being a virgin when they marry.'

He exploded out of his seat, then remembered he was supposed to be acting out the concerned friend, rather than overheated would-be lover. Making a calming gesture with his hands, intended for himself as much as anyone, he turned to Jazz. 'Forgive me, Jazz. This is none of my business, but I didn't know men still made that type of demand on a woman. This must be hard for you, impossible to talk about with me around…' He turned for the door, desperate to kick it in, or smash a fist into a block of wood.

'No, stay,' Jazz said quietly. 'You might as well know everything.'

Too right. He leaned back against the door. 'OK.' He remained outwardly calm, while a firestorm of concern for Jazz kicked off inside him. What kind of Neanderthal was she planning to marry? And when had this been settled? Last he'd heard, talks between the emir and Sharif were just getting started.

'Jazz must do what's right for her,' his peace-making sister Leila insisted. 'None of us has any idea what it takes to be a princess of Kareshi.' Turning to Jazz, she added, 'And we'll support you in whatever you decide to do.'

Jazz stood up too. 'I know you will.' She was clearly moved by their concern. 'Will you all excuse me for a moment?'

'Of course.' The chorus of Skavangas was unanimous.

Tyr stood aside to let Jazz go, but he didn't give his sisters a chance to reinforce the message the three of them were so urgently firing at him. He was going to do something about this, and was on it before Jazz had closed the door.

He closed it for her—with them both on the same side.

'What are you doing?' Jazz gasped, staring up at him in alarm as he shut the door behind them.

He came straight to the point. 'Have you thought this through?'

Jazz stared down at his hands on her arm, and for a very dangerous moment passions ran as high between them as they had way back when. Anything might have happened in those few, potent seconds, but then Jazz drew in a shaky breath and the torment in her eyes made him let her go. As his hands dropped to his side, she whispered, 'Leila's right. I know you don't understand this, but I have to at least consider the emir's offer, because of all the benefits it could bring to Kareshi.'

'Nonsense! I told you before, this isn't right for you, and you know it, Jazz. I can see it on your face.'

'I knew I should have come veiled,' she murmured dryly, the old Jazz peeping through.

Somehow that flash of spirit made it all the harder to come to terms with this.

'Don't joke, Jazz. This is your life we're talking about.'

'Exactly, Tyr.' Her chin tipped up. Steel entered her voice. 'This is my life. Now, will you please let me go?'

She stared past him to the bathroom and he stood aside. Grinding his jaw, he watched her go, wondering how he was going to live with himself if he did as Jazz asked—stood back and did nothing.

Jazz left them soon after that, kissing and hugging his sisters goodbye, but barely acknowledging Tyr. She had somewhere to be quite urgently, he gathered. The rest of the afternoon was spent in stormy silence. He turned up the volume on the match, while his sisters talked in undertones at the table. He had no more interest in their conversation. He knew what they were talking about. He knew how he felt about it. And he was damned if was going to share those feelings with anyone.

He didn't move until his mobile phone rang and then he took the call in the other room.

'Sharif? There's nothing wrong, is there?' The line was bad. He was instantly concerned.

'Yes and no. I need you out in Kareshi, Tyr.'

His thought processes raced. Kareshi? Jazz. Yes. *Yes* had to be his answer to Sharif's request.

'Sorry to rush you back there, Tyr—no, there's nothing wrong,' Sharif confirmed to his relief. 'Had to leave unexpectedly. No problem. Just some business to attend to.'

'I understand.' He relaxed. Sharif was obviously travelling where a good line wasn't always a given.

'The Wadi villagers have called for help in getting their Internet connection established, and they need someone to show them how to use it. I wouldn't ask you to go back right away, but I can't send anyone they don't know. They've been so isolated up to now and they trust you.'

He frowned as he remembered his promise to return to Wadi village as soon as he had made his peace with his sisters. 'I won't let them down.'

'Soon?' Sharif asked cryptically.

'Tomorrow soon enough for you?'

'Tomorrow is perfect.'

Britt's face was rigid when he returned to the sitting room. 'Leave it, Tyr.'

'Leave what?' His thoughts were racing with plans for his return to Kareshi, and the chance to see Jazz again, on her home ground, where they could continue this discussion. When Jazz had talked about freedom, she had envisaged the type of freedom everyone in this room took for granted. He couldn't just sit here. He had to do something.

'Leave this business with Jazz alone,' Britt insisted when he stonewalled her with a look. 'And don't tell me you're not thinking about her. I know that look. You seem to think Jazz was forced into making this decision.'

'A decision she hasn't seen through yet,' he pointed out, 'so there's still time for her to change her mind, and if I see her in Kareshi I will certainly say something.'

'Are you suggesting Sharif would force Jazz into doing something she doesn't want to?' Britt demanded.

As passions between them grew heated, Leila

stepped in. 'No, of course Tyr isn't saying that, Britt.' And gradually, like a pan of boiling milk taken off the heat, everyone calmed down again.

Until Eva chipped in with, 'You should tell him, Britt.'

He spun round. 'Tell me what?'

'I know you just spoke to Sharif,' Britt began, haltingly for her, he thought. 'Sharif told me he was going to ring you—'

'And?' he flashed.

'Calm down, Tyr. Give me chance to explain.' Britt's face was white with tension. Nothing about this situation was easy for her. 'Jazz won't be in Kareshi when you get back,' she explained, 'and you'll probably have left the country before she arrives. And, before you ask, she isn't in Skavanga, either.'

'She was here earlier,' he protested.

'And now she's gone,' Britt confirmed.

'Gone? Gone where?'

'Jazz has left Skavanga with Sharif.'

His mind reeled. Just when he thought he might get the chance to talk some sense into Jazz, she had left Skavanga for some destination unknown.

Unless—

'Tell me she hasn't gone to Qadar.' His muscles tensed as he waited for one of his sisters to answer.

'No,' Britt reassured him. 'And before you get angry, I think this might be my fault. Sharif and I talked about getting Jazz out of Kareshi so she can get a fresh perspective on life, so instead of leaving Skavanga for Kareshi as Jazz had planned, Sharif has laid on a treat for her. He's not happy with Jazz falling meekly into line with the traditionalists in Kareshi, either. He doesn't see Jazz as a docile princess. He never has.'

'Jazz—docile?' He grimaced at the thought. 'So where's he taken her?'

'To the fashion shows in Milan.'

'To the fashion shows?' He laughed out loud. No wonder Britt couldn't look at him. 'To the *fashion* shows?' he repeated. 'Does Sharif know anything about his sister?'

Ignoring Britt's protests, he made an angry gesture. 'Since when has Jazz been a front-row fashionista? Jazz is happiest out in the desert, riding free.'

'Tyr.' Leila followed him to the door. 'Don't

do anything hasty. It won't help Jazz. Sharif was looking for something to take Jazz's mind off the emir and his proposal. It will at least give her a chance to think things through calmly before she agrees to something she might regret for the rest of her life.'

'But I haven't had a chance to say goodbye to her.'

'You sound so lost,' Leila observed, touching his arm.

And angry, he thought, ashamed he'd sounded off as he stared down at his heavily pregnant sister. 'I'm acting like a bear with a sore head. I just can't get my head around Jazz's crazy life choices. You know I'm never angry with you, Leila.'

'I know that.' Leila smiled in sympathy, then exclaimed, 'Where are you going?' as he moved past her towards the door.

'I'm not sure yet,' he said honestly. 'But I promise to keep in touch this time, okay?'

He had not expected Leila to stand in his way. Drawing her into a reassuring hug, he kissed the top of her head. He hated leaving his sisters like this, but they had husbands to take care of them and Jazz had no one.

No one apart from an army of heavily armed bodyguards sent by Sharif to watch her every move, he guessed. Once again, Jazz would be shielded from reality, and from life itself, so what chance did she stand of making an informed choice about her future?

CHAPTER SIX

SHE'D HAD THIS crazy idea that if she stayed out of the way until the links with Qadar were safely established and the final arrangements for her wedding to the emir were in place, it would be too late for her to do anything about it. The decision would be taken out of her hands. All good for Kareshi. Borders secured for all time through her marriage to the emir.

But when you put three Skavanga sisters into the mix, with Britt's business brain calling foul on the suggested arrangement between a very wealthy Kareshi and a less well-off Qadar, and Eva ranting that no one in their right minds could possibly want to spend the rest of their lives with a man they hadn't even been to bed with, backed up by a chorus of concern from Leila, you were left, not with a melodious chorus of agreement and support for her decision, but with a rowdy chorus of dissent.

And then there was Tyr.

And Sharif.

And the fact that, far from being happy on her tiny gilt chair squashed in between all the heavy hitters and fashion press in the front row of every show in town, Jazz was thoroughly fed up. If she had to watch another unlined, asymmetric rag passing itself off as a work of art, she might have to resort to wearing a hemp sack for her wedding.

Her wedding.

It was definitely time to go back to Kareshi before she lost her nerve to go ahead with what she still stubbornly believed was the best thing she could do for her country. Wedding negotiations between Kareshi and Qadar must be close to complete by now, surely? And even that sounded wrong. How could two countries get married?

She was planning to marry a country?

Heaving a sigh so loud it made Jazz's neighbours on the gilt chairs turn to look at her with surprise, she confronted the marriage plans she'd thought made such sense and realised they were full of holes. How could she help her country if she was stuck away in Qadar? She needed to get away from the flashing lights and loud music to the quiet of the desert, where she could rethink her plans for the future. Bringing out her phone, she was just about to start making travel plans when a message from Eva flashed up.

Tyr is working at Wadi village.

And?

And good morning to you, Princess Prim.

Eva? What do you want me to say???

Is sexual frustration hindering your ability to think straight? If so, please call this helpline now—

EVA!

Just thought you'd like to know. Fashion shows treating you well?

Zzzzzzzzzz

Why are you still there?

My thoughts exactly.

Jazz paused a moment before asking the question drumming at her mind.

What's Tyr doing in Kareshi?

Not looking for a patsy to perform the dance of the seven veils for him in his harem like the Evil Emu of Qadar, that's for sure.

EVA!!

What good are you to Kareshi if you're trussed up in feather handcuffs?

Not sure the emir would go for that.

Are you prepared to take that chance?

There was a long pause while Jazz digested this and squirmed uncomfortably on her chair.

OK, I give in. *big sigh* Tyr's setting up an Internet connection at Wadi village, so if you hurry...

What's that got to do with me?

He needs fizzers and gum to keep him sane. You can take them with you.

But I'm not going to Wadi village.

Yes, you are.

There was a very long pause and then Jazz tapped in a message.

Miss you, Eva.

Miss you too, brown eyes. See you in Kareshi?

Never say never to a billowing Bedouin tent ☺ xx

She could be part of Eva's world, and part of the new world Sharif was working so hard to build in Kareshi, or she could become Princess Prim—embittered old spinster, twisting around in her own web of gloom, Jazz concluded as she put her phone back in her bag. The alternative was marriage to a man she didn't know. And if the emir did decide to shut her away in his harem, Eva was right: What use would she be to Kareshi then?

The least Eva had done was make her think. Excusing herself politely before the lights went up on the second half of the show, Jazz picked up the hem of her flowing silk robe to brave the hazard of big bags and small feet as she made her escape from fashion fantasy island to the reality she had been avoiding for far too long.

Jazz knew she had made the right decision in coming back to Kareshi the moment the royal helicopter lifted her high above the rolling plain of verdant green immediately surrounding Sharif's principal palace smack bang in the middle of the desert. 'A garden in the desert' was how the world's press described this area, and that was all thanks to her brother's vision.

Sharif was her idol. Her brother was Kareshi's idol, and one day she hoped to equal his achievements.

And she wouldn't do that in Qadar.

But she still had that niggling sense of guilt, because she had always chosen duty over self-indulgence every time, and coming back here to Kareshi seemed like the biggest self-indulgence of all when there was nowhere else on earth she would rather be. But if, by staying in Kareshi as the unmarried sister of the sheikh, she became a burden to Sharif, she would never forgive herself. So, wouldn't it be easier to go along with the emir's plan?

Easy was not an option for Jazz Kareshi, or for her brother, Jazz reminded herself. When Sharif took the throne there had been endless conflict until he proved himself a worthy leader. Their dream was for all the people of Kareshi to live together in harmony, and now Jazz wondered if perhaps she had taken her personal crusade a step too far. Sharif had never asked her to appease the traditionalists by marrying the ultra-conservative Emir of Qadar. When had that idea seemed the only sensible solution? Now she was back in Kareshi, the answer seemed clear. She had to stay here, to work here; this was where she belonged.

As she rested back in her seat to consider this change of plan, the royal helicopter soared high over Wadi village, where Eva had said Tyr was staying.

Tyr.

Tyr had a special affinity with the desert that had brought them together when they were young. Staring down through the always disturbingly see-through Perspex floor beneath her feet, she wondered what he was doing and if he was alone. Tyr shouldn't be alone. The shadows behind his eyes called for friendship and support to remove them. She had to thank Eva for rattling her out of going down the wrong path and bringing her back here. There were people who needed her far more than the Emir of Qadar. People like Tyr, whose soul was wounded, and who had returned to find peace in the vastness of the desert and real purpose in his work. She would like to help him, but would he let her?

Shifting position, Jazz knew she had to stop dreaming about Tyr Skavanga and what he meant to her. They had both moved on, and Tyr had made it clear at the party that he didn't want or need her company. She couldn't save the world—not even her own small part of it, let alone get to the bottom of those shadows behind Tyr's eyes.

But that wouldn't stop her trying, and it wouldn't stop her dreaming, either. And dreams had to be big, or what was the point in having them? If Tyr Skavanga was working at Wadi village, she was bound to see him. She often rode out that way.

As the helicopter came in to land, she accepted that it might be necessary to trim her dreams to fit reality. Even if he were interested, Tyr would want more from a woman than a shrinking virgin, and Jazz dreaded the reality of sex. Somehow marriage to a man she didn't know had held far less fear than any physical association with someone she did know, perhaps because marriage to the emir had always had an air of unreality about it.

While Tyr Skavanga in all his randy, delicious state was all too real.

That evening with Tyr at the party had sent her primal senses rocketing off the scale, because even she could sense that Tyr was a highly sexed hunter in the prime of his life, while she was a virgin who knew nothing about sex, except in theory. And what she'd heard was hardly enticing—except when Eva got started, but then Eva had always liked to shock, so it was never possible to be sure if what Eva said was absolutely true.

'You can take your safety belt off now, Princess Jasmina.'

The pilot's voice sounded shrill and metallic in her headphones as he switched off the engine, and she bit back a smile at the thought of how lucky she was that he couldn't read her thoughts. She'd keep her safety belt well and truly fastened until the day she got married, thank you very much.

Tyr was coated in sand from head to foot after trekking for hours over rugged terrain. There had been a shift in the pattern of the sand dunes since the last storm, meaning the four-wheel drive couldn't take him any closer to the village. He'd radioed to make sure the vehicle could be collected before the next storm closed in, and then he set out on foot. It was a relief to know Jazz was half a world away with this bad storm closing in.

Pausing to shift his backpack into a more comfortable position, he thought back to his school-days, when Sharif had taken pity on him during the holidays because Tyr had three sisters. But when Tyr had arrived in the desert he had discovered that his troubles had only just begun, because Sharif's one sister had been more aggravation than his three put together. At first he'd thought it would be an easy matter to shake Jazz off when she tagged along, but they hadn't had a horse fast enough to get away from her. They'd devised all sorts of cunning plans, but Jazz had always outrun them. They'd be relaxing beside the oasis while their horses drank their fill when she'd appear round a palm tree to taunt them, until finally they gave in, and their exclusive gang of two became three.

Cresting the dune overlooking Wadi village, he stared down as if he expected to see Jazz waiting for him. Of course she wasn't there. She was in Milan, pretending to be a fashionista. And even if she had been waiting for him, they could never recapture those innocent days. Time had changed them both too much for that. Squinting his eyes against the low-lying rays of a dying sun, he set out on the last leg of his journey.

Had she ever been so happy to tug on riding gear?

Nope, Jazz concluded, not even bothering to check her appearance in the mirror. The sun was up and the grey light of dawn was slowly giving way to a warm buttery glow. It promised to be a fabulous day for riding, if she got out before the sun rose too high, turning everything from comfortably warm into the fiery pit of hell. With her hair tied neatly back, and her close-fitting breeches covered by one of the long, concealing shirts she wore for riding, she only had to pick up her hard hat at the door and she was ready to trial her new stallion. Spear was said to be impossible to ride. She'd see about that. Kindness combined with firmness always won the day with a difficult stallion, and Spear was such a beautiful beast.

Now, why should Tyr Skavanga flash into her mind?

Where beautiful beasts were concerned, Tyr was a prime example, that was why.

Maybe she'd catch sight of Tyr if she rode by Wadi village.

She was a princess with responsibilities—she had to remember that.

Okay, so she wouldn't go that way, not unless the wind blew from the east, in which case she didn't want the sand in her face, and so then she would have no option but to turn in the direction of Wadi village.

Leaving her bedroom, Jazz raced down the stairs and minutes later she was in the stable yard. Crossing to the half-open door, she whispered to Spear and caressed his ears, for which she received a whinnying reply and a good nuzzle as the horse set about searching her pockets for mints. Resting her cheek against his warm, firm muscular neck, she revelled in the stallion's tightly contained strength, and her thoughts flew back to Tyr. What was he doing now? Would he be thinking about her?

Don't be ridiculous!

But there was a chance Tyr might be preparing to ride out. Dawn and dusk had always been his favourite times to ride too, because dawn was so beautifully still and silent, while dusk was cool.

Talking quietly to her horse, Jazz led her magnificent stallion into the yard. 'You are a bad boy,' Jazz breathed as the stallion threw back his head, resisting her attempts to calm him, 'but you're very handsome,' she soothed as she sprang lightly into the saddle. The stallion was impatient for his morning run and skittered sideways until she brought him back under control. Shifting her weight, she coaxed him forward at a controlled canter, rather than the flat-out gallop Spear was aiming for.

Having passed beneath the stone archway that divided the safe, controlled environment of Sharif's racing stables from the desert beyond, they entered the wild, unpredictable frontier, as Jazz always thought of her desert home, and, drawing in a deep breath of joyful anticipation, she lightened her grip and gave Spear his head.

The wind ripped her veil off as she galloped across the dunes. She was at one with the powerful beast as he surged forward, and that was the best sensation in the world. Spear had exceeded all her expectations and anyone who said she couldn't ride him because he was too strong for her was so wrong. She could do anything if she put her mind to it, and Spear was perfection. It was just a pity about the wind. Blowing from the east, it gave her only one option, which was to head in the direction of Wadi village.

She decided to take a short cut. It was a riskier route than going round the dunes, but much quicker. The climb up the final dune was the most testing, but when she reached the top she could see the oasis where she had used to swim with Tyr, and Wadi village, spread out like a twinkling toy city in front of her.

The cold water of the oasis hitting his heated skin was a pleasure Tyr had anticipated since the moment he woke up. There was nowhere else on earth like this; nowhere that assaulted his senses quite so comprehensively with such contrasts of hot and cold, shade and light, and sheer vastness. Everything was extreme in the desert. That was why he liked it. There were no grey areas. There was just constant challenge and danger. Easing his shoulders, he prepared to dive in.

And was stopped by a shriek.

Swinging round, he saw the stallion's legs

buckle beneath it as it started the long slide down the dune. It was a relief to see the rider instinctively kick away the stirrups and leap off its back to avoid being crushed beneath half a ton of horse. Recognising the rider, he grabbed a towel and began to run.

'Jazz!'

He powered up the bank of the oasis. The next few seconds passed in a disorientating blur of sand and spinning horse as Jazz and her stallion rocketed down the slope. He jumped clear as the horse skidded past him with its legs pounding uselessly at the air. Jazz took a little longer to arrive, before landing at his feet in an untidy sprawl. Hunkering down, he made a quick assessment. She was winded. She was shocked. She couldn't speak. Apart from that, her colour was good and she was breathing, always a plus.

'Tyr?'

Letting go of her hand, he sat back on his heels.

'My horse?' she gasped out.

'Unharmed.' He glanced at the banks of the oasis, where he could see Jazz's horse sucking in water. 'Are you okay?' He sounded gruff and guessed he was probably more shocked than Jazz. 'Aren't you supposed to be swanning around in Italy, buying next year's thrift-shop donations?'

'Sorry?' She gave him a look that came straight from the old days. 'Did I get off at the wrong stop?'

Hiding a smile, he stared sternly down at her. 'This could have been a really serious accident, and we still don't know if you've been hurt.'

'Only my pride,' she admitted, struggling to get up.

He pressed her down. 'You're not going anywhere until I check you over for injury. And, apologies in advance, but I will have to touch you.'

'No, you won't,' Jazz flashed, doing her best to roll out of reach.

'For purely medical reasons,' he said, patiently bringing her back again. 'Believe me, I have no wish to do this.'

Much. His fingers were on fire at the thought.

CHAPTER SEVEN

JAZZ BRACED HERSELF as she prepared for Tyr to conduct his examination. Closing her eyes, she turned her head away, as if to show him that if she must endure this personal invasion, she would do so while distanced from him in both thought and response. This was something new for him, and he wasn't sure whether to be offended or amused by a woman who didn't want him to touch her. He made the exam swift, gentling his big hands as much as he could, but Jazz felt so good beneath his touch, he found it almost impossible to remain clinically objective.

'Is this really necessary?' she demanded at one point when his fingertips scraped her breast.

'Bruised ribs,' he said tersely, consciously steadying his breathing. 'I'm checking they're not broken.'

'What about the new medical facility in the village? Can't I get checked over there?'

The new medical facility he had only recently installed? Now, why hadn't he thought of that? 'I'm just making sure it's safe to move you first.'

'It's safe.' Jazz's eyes flashed fire. 'And as soon as I've had chance to catch my breath, I'm standing up.'

'And I'll help you,' he said calmly. Straightening her shirt, he hunkered back on his heels to wait.

This was not the way she'd planned it. This was supposed to be an innocent morning ride. And, okay, if it had turned into a scouting mission, she hadn't expected such immediate and intimate contact with her target. Having Tyr loom over her while she was lying prone on the ground was having all sorts of odd effects on her body, none of them welcome.

'If that snake hadn't slithered in front of my horse…'

'You'd still be up there, spying on me swimming naked in the oasis?'

'Certainly not!' She tried to get up, but Tyr pushed her down again. 'I didn't even know you were there,' she defended, studiously ignoring his towel-clad frame. She absolutely refused to notice his biceps, or his formidable torso, or any other part of him that was currently brazenly on show. 'I was taking my horse for a drink, and that's all.'

'You certainly picked a safe way down,' Tyr remarked, his voice dripping with irony.

'Past a snake,' she reminded him acidly.

'End result? You're lying in a heap at my feet.'

'A heap? I'll have you know, I'm still in shock.'

'Of course you are.'

'And don't you dare look at me like that.'

'Like what?' Tyr demanded as he unfolded his massive frame.

'As if I'm today's entertainment. And don't stand over me, either.'

'You're right. I'll have to carry you back to the village.'

'What? You can't do that.' Scrambling to her feet, she promptly fell down again.

Luckily, Tyr caught her before she hit the ground. He propped her against the sturdy trunk of a palm and stood back. 'Stay there while I put some clothes on.'

Shivers of awareness raced through her as she closed her eyes.

A pair of snug-fitting jeans, some desert boots and a black top later, Tyr returned. 'Here's what's going to happen, Princess. You may or may not have concussion, so you're not walking back to the village.' He held up his hand when she began to protest. 'You can do what the hell you want once the doctors have checked you over, but until then you're under orders—*my* orders.'

Her jaw dropped with astonishment. Her body might have other ideas, but she wasn't completely mad. 'I forbid you to touch me.'

'You forbid me?' Tyr laughed. Then he swung her into his arms.

At some point she realised that the more she struggled, the more her body approved as it rubbed against Tyr's, so she made herself as stiff as a plank. But this was no longer a game, and the implications of arriving in a conservative village in the arms of a man didn't bear thinking about. 'Tyr. Please. You can't carry me into Wadi village.'

'Watch me.'

'You don't understand. Some of the most conservative people in Kareshi live in Wadi village.'

'I understand everything, Jazz. You forget, I've been working in the village for quite some time.'

'Then please put me down.'

'I won't take that risk with your safety.' Ignoring her increasingly strident protests, Tyr continued on along the bank of the oasis, where he only paused to gather up her horse's reins before turning in the direction of the village.

She made one final attempt to make him change his mind. 'Please, Tyr. Put me down. I can ride back.'

'You're in no fit state to ride back. Look at you. You're shaking.' Halting mid-stride, Tyr blazed a stare into her face, his expression fixed and determined. 'What am I supposed to do? Leave you here to fry?'

'That might be better.' But then she glanced up at the sky, which was rapidly changing from cloudless blue to sun-bleached white. Death was better than disgrace, right? she reasoned frantically—which made her wonder briefly if she did indeed have concussion.

'How would it look to the people of Wadi village if I leave you in the desert to die?' Tyr demanded, distracting her. 'Let me tell you,' he said before she had chance to reply. 'It would look as if the man who has been working with them, the same man the villagers have grown to trust, is nothing but a barbarian who holds life cheap, and who shows total disrespect for their royal family. You've had a fall. We don't know if you're injured yet. At the very least, you've sustained a shock. In the absence of an ambulance rumbling over the dunes, I'm carrying you back to the medical centre, where you can be checked out and treated. Anyone on earth would understand that.'

'My people won't.'

'Your people would rather have you dead?' Tyr shook his head. 'You don't know them, Jazz. They love you. They talk about you and Sharif constantly. Together you've brought stability to Kareshi. You must never take a chance like that again. What if I hadn't planned to swim in the oasis? What if you'd broken your leg and were stranded out here? What if your horse had run away? Are you carrying a satellite phone or a tracking device?'

In her rush to see Tyr, she had remembered none of these things, Jazz realised, but that wasn't something she was about to share with him. 'They must have been lost during the fall.'

'Yeah, right.' He strode on.

Her heart sank. They had almost reached the outskirts of the village, and people were already coming out of their houses to take a look. Smiling grimly as he reassured people in broken Kareshi, Tyr continued on through the crowd. He either didn't know or didn't care that touching her was practically a criminal offence. And she couldn't blame the villagers for their concern. Before Tyr had arrived on the scene, installing the Internet and bringing fresh water to the village, they hadn't met a stranger for goodness knew how long. They led remote, sheltered lives, shielded from the world, with traditions that had remained unchanged for centuries. How long before news of her unconventional arrival flashed around Kareshi? She smiled in an attempt to reassure the veiled women, whose eyes were wide with concern for her, and nodded briefly at the men, who turned away. She was shamed in their eyes, and no excuse could possibly explain her outlandish behaviour.

Pausing only to hand over the reins of her horse to one of the young boys who had been following them, Tyr carried her inside the clinic, where he handed her over to the orderlies like a parcel he was glad to be rid of. There was nothing wrong with his manner towards her. There was nothing but pure concern in his eyes, though Jazz doubted the traditionalists would see it that way.

'I'm going to check on your horse,' he called back as he left the building.

'Thank you.' She was uncomfortably aware of the increasing clamour of the crowd outside the clinic as the people waited for news of their princess.

'I must go to them and explain,' she told the nurse, struggling into a sitting position.

The nurse gently pushed her down again. 'We can do that for you,' she said firmly. 'Forgive me, Princess Jasmina, but you're not going anywhere until the doctor's had chance to take a look at you. You might as well rest back. There's nothing for you to worry about. His Majesty has already been informed.'

Great! Jazz's breath left her body in a shuddering sigh. She could imagine Sharif's reaction. Having had her beg him to arrange a marriage for her, he now discovered she was here with Tyr.

Needless to say, by the time the nurse took her blood pressure, it was sky-high. The nurse peered at her over her spectacles. 'Even if the doctor gives his okay, I'm going to insist that you stay here and rest. This equipment tells me you've been badly shaken up.'

And not just by the fall from her horse, Jazz thought.

Tyr needed space from Jazz and time to think. He still hadn't got over the shock of finding her here in Kareshi, and now there was the sensation he'd caused to deal with on top of that. He wouldn't risk losing the people's trust. Nor did he want to damage his friendship with Sharif. Taking some of the elders aside, he decided to sort it out.

Their reaction threw him.

'No, no, no,' he said, smiling as he shook his head to make his position clear. 'We're not planning to get married.'

'But you must,' the headman said in a tone that brooked no argument.

Tyr was still smiling, still convinced that this couldn't be a serious suggestion on the part of the headman, but his laughing gaze was met by an unwavering stare. 'All right.' Taking it in good part, he clapped the old man on the back. 'We'll sort this out—

'Apparently not,' Tyr murmured as the old man walked away. 'Later,' he called after him.

The headman raised his hand, but only in acknowledgement that he'd heard Tyr, and nothing more.

He got a really bad feeling. That encounter with the headman of the village had suggested that nothing would yield to good humour in this situation. And in truth, fudging an issue wasn't his style. He was straight down the line. So far he'd done nothing to let these people down and he wasn't about to start now.

He placed a call to Sharif, but couldn't get through. Leading his horse out of its stable, he sprang onto its back and headed out of the village. This was a mess that should never have happened. Jazz Kareshi, innocent princess, and the ruthless killing machine? If her people knew his history, would they be so keen to make a match between them? He couldn't do that to Jazz, so the only thing he could do was to leave Kareshi.

And how was he going to do that, when he was tied by his love for the people? His work here wasn't done.

As each insoluble point jabbed at his mind, he spurred his horse on until they were racing at a flat-out gallop. He only reined in when he spotted a Bedouin encampment in the shadow of the dunes. Changing his balance, he slowed the horse. For a while he just let the reins hang loose as he watched the people going about their daily lives. The Bedouin were purposeful and contented. He had always envied the nomadic lifestyle, and it was only recently that he'd lost the urge to move on. He loved the desert, and he wouldn't abandon Jazz, not when he was responsible for the situation she was in. He would stay and see this out, and when everything had settled down again—

He'd turn his back on Jazz and leave?

That was the safest thing to do. Safest for Jazz.

Turning his horse, he headed back to the village. The only thing he could be sure about was that he wasn't going anywhere until this mess was sorted out.

CHAPTER EIGHT

AS SOON AS the doctor said she could go and the nurse released her, Jazz called the palace to arrange for the helicopter to pick her up and for her wilful, snake-shy stallion to be collected. She could have ridden him back if the nurse hadn't mentioned a storm closing in. She wouldn't risk her horse, so it was down to hoping the weather would hold long enough for the helicopter to fly in, and then back again to the palace.

And now she was grateful to the women of the village for being so kind to her. After standing vigil outside the medical facility, they insisted on taking Jazz to the unmarried women's quarters, where they said she'd be safe until the helicopter came to take her home. Having grown up with her brother in the palace, she found it a fascinating experience to be drawn into village life. Everyone was so friendly, and it made her think again how much she had missed female companionship, and how her life could change for the better if she only allowed it to. She'd had the warmth and friendship of the Skavanga sisters since Britt married Sharif, and she could have the friendship of these people too, if she stayed in Kareshi.

Once inside the women's pavilion, it surprised Jazz to see that, along with the more traditional trappings she might have expected, like silken cushions and low brass tables bearing platters of fruit and jugs of freshly squeezed juice, a large space had been allocated to a bank of computer screens faced by no-nonsense office chairs.

'Our benefactor is Tyr Skavanga,' one of the women explained, her sloe eyes warm with admiration behind the traditional veil. 'He bought all the equipment and installed it for us. It's like a miracle. The world comes to us. We can even Internet shop.'

As the women started to laugh, Jazz joined in the fun, but it did make her wonder if she was the only one being left behind where progress was concerned.

'Distance learning,' the same woman explained, jolting Jazz back to the present.

They joined a group of women clustered around a screen. 'We all want to be able to work like you, Princess Jasmina,' a young girl exclaimed, springing up.

'Please, won't you sit down again?' Jazz insisted. 'I'm here to learn all I can from you.'

Reassured, the girl continued, 'Thanks to this link with the outside world, set up by Tyr Skavanga, we can learn to become the teachers of the future.'

Tyr Skavanga...Tyr Skavanga...

And there was so much to do here—so much enthusiasm for progress surrounding her. What was she thinking? Leave Kareshi? Was she mad? What was she so afraid of? Tyr at the party flashed into her head; Tyr rescuing her after the fall from her horse; Tyr—

Just Tyr, Jazz realised, because Tyr represented a time that was lost, and everything she feared about the future. It wasn't Tyr's fault he was so brutally masculine, but, though she was bold in every other area of her life, Jazz had always had a fear of men and sex—Tyr and sex—because all she knew about sex was colourful and sometimes terrifying rumour.

As the women continued to chat easily to her, Jazz knew exactly what she had to do—and it didn't include the Emir of Qadar. Sharif would be mad with her for wasting his time and she couldn't blame him. There would be diplomatic repercussions, but this was where she belonged. She could be of some real help to her brother here.

And then the bombshell dropped.

Another, bolder girl asked Jazz how she had dared to love an outsider.

All the women went quiet as they waited for her answer.

'An outsider?' Jazz queried cautiously.

'Tyr Skavanga,' the women prompted in a laughing chorus, as if this were obvious to everyone except Jazz.

Jazz laughed too. 'I don't love Tyr like that,' she protested, maybe a little too heartily. 'We've been friends since childhood. And, yes, I admire Tyr, but that's as far as it goes.'

The women seemed unconvinced. No wonder, when her cheeks burned red. They were determined to believe she was involved in a runaway romance like the films they'd been able to watch on the Internet, thanks to their benefactor, Tyr Skavanga.

And then one of the older women took her aside. 'Just think of it,' she said. 'You have already proved your worth to your brother, His Majesty, by improving the management of his racing stables. Imagine what you could do for us in Kareshi with Tyr Skavanga organising the various building programmes, while you recruit and manage the staff?'

'What? I—? Oh, no.' But it was a seductive thought, though what Tyr would make of it, she didn't like to think.

Things couldn't get any worse. Tyr was still miles from the village with a sandstorm coming. All flights were grounded. No one would be flying in or out of Wadi village any time soon to rescue Princess Jasmina. All communication links were down, and no one could predict how long the storm would last. Sensing danger approaching, his horse had started to play up, which was why he was on foot. Having tied his bandana over the animal's eyes, he was coaxing it forward inch by torturous inch, his muscles bulging at the strain of persuading the horse to lift its hooves out of the treacherously shifting sand. He could only hope Jazz was safely housed in the village by now. He was impatient to get back and make sure of it.

The sky was an ominous greenish-yellow by the time he made it back to the village. Having fed and watered his horse, he went to find Jazz. It was his duty to do so, he told himself firmly. He found her in the village hall, where she was taking note of people's concerns. Typical Jazz—no time like the present, even with a sandstorm brewing. She was fully veiled in deference to the traditionalists, but, even with only her expressive eyes on show, he could see enough to want her in a way he was more than certain the elders of the village would not approve of. And then she saw him and her eyes crinkled slightly. The tightening in his groin was immediate, and it was almost a relief when she turned away.

Watching Jazz amongst her people only reinforced his opinion that Jazz was needed right here in Kareshi, not in Qadar. Jazz Kareshi was one of the most valuable resources Kareshi possessed. There wasn't a single doubt in his mind that Jazz belonged with her people.

How much more they could accomplish if they worked together.

Thoughts like that led nowhere. If they saw each other on a regular basis and he infected an innocent young girl like Jazz with his darkness, what then?

As it happened, Jazz took the decision out of his hands by approaching him, and, in spite of all his self-imposed warning, his heart warmed when Jazz stared up at him.

'You're back.'

For a few potent moments she stared into his eyes.

'If you need me, Jazz, you only have to ask.'

'As it happens…'

He followed her gaze to the bank of computers he'd installed, which were currently standing idle.

'While I take a note of everyone's concerns, you could show those who don't know how to use the computers,' she suggested.

'You want me to teach school?'

'Why not?' She gave him a look. 'That's if you're up to it.'

He held her gaze. 'I think I can handle it. Though I'm pretty sure the Internet's down.'

'No excuses, Tyr. You can still show people plenty without it.'

'Whatever you say, Princess.'

Did Tyr have to lower his voice and stare quite so intently into her eyes? Jazz glanced around to make sure no one had noticed.

'There's no point sitting around doing nothing as we wait for the storm to pass,' she pointed out. 'The children are bored, and this is a great opportunity for those who want to benefit from your expertise.'

Her heart raced as Tyr raised a mocking brow. 'Would you like to benefit from my expertise too, Princess? Or are you already a computer expert?'

She let a shaking breath out with relief, and then noticed Tyr's eyes were warm and teasing, as they had used to be when they were kids. 'Just pretend you know what you're doing,' she suggested.

'Oh, I know what I'm doing, Princess.'

There was something in Tyr's tone that made her suck in a fast breath. She pushed it aside by raising her voice so everyone could hear.

'Tyr has offered to help anyone interested in learning more about computers.'

The stampede made him smile. He'd been leaning against the wall with all his attention fixed on Jazz, but she'd stitched him up good and tight. She didn't know how good she was, he reflected as he watched her settling people down in front of the screens. And her spirit had definitely returned in Wadi village. The people loved her, but, more importantly, Jazz was gaining in confidence all the time. The people trusted Jazz, and responded to her. They confided things they would never dream of confiding to a court official, let alone Jazz's brother, Sharif. This was where Jazz belonged, and he could only be thankful that she was beginning to see that for herself.

And how about his pledge to stay away from her?

He glanced outside at the whirling sand. How was he supposed to predict they'd be sharing an enclosed space like this?

'They like you,' Jazz remarked to him when they broke for refreshments.

'Don't sound so surprised. I have been working here in the village for quite some time now.'

'But I am surprised. You're really good at this, Tyr. And here was me, thinking you were a confirmed loner.'

'I am, but we're trapped by the storm,' he pointed out.

Jazz was so enthused, she wasn't even listening. 'What we need is a new school and more teachers. I put that in my last mail to Sharif, so I hope we get an answer from him as soon as this storm eases up a bit. Everyone's so eager to learn.'

He smiled as he listened to Jazz spelling out her plan. His thoughts were somewhat less innocent. There was only one woman in this room he wanted to teach, and those lessons would have nothing to do with computer skills.

He glanced outside at the rapidly darkening sky. 'I'm going to call a halt soon, Jazz,' he said, breaking her off. 'I want everyone safely under cover before this storm gets any worse. It's going to be bad, so I'll see the elderly home, and then come back for you.'

She bridled at that suggestion. 'I'm quite capable of looking after myself, Tyr.'

'Are you? Would that be the same way you looked after yourself when you were out riding?'

Feeling her bristle, he drew the back of his hand down her arm to lighten the atmosphere. He could not have anticipated Jazz's response. To say she recoiled in horror was putting it mildly.

'Haven't you heard a word I've said, Tyr? You *must not* touch me.'

The skin around Jazz's eyes had paled to ivory, but her eyes were almost solid black. He'd seen that same reaction before in a woman, but never in a situation like this. Passions were certainly roused. No one was looking, but anyone would think he had cupped Jazz's breast, or worse. How innocent was she, exactly? Utterly innocent of all things sexual, he concluded as Jazz continued to glare at him.

'I'll see the children home,' she said sharply, and with a swish of her veil she was gone from his side, but before she could round up her flock, the headman called the meeting to order.

Tyr shrugged and threw Jazz a rueful smile when she was forced back into his company.

'No hope of the helicopter arriving to save me from you, I suppose?' she gritted out during a lull in the proceedings.

He held her gaze and saw her eyes grow black. 'Not a chance. The forecast is grim. Nothing's coming in or out of here today.'

Including us, Jazz's worried eyes seemed to say. 'Did you manage to speak to Sharif?' she asked.

'No. Did you get hold of him?'

Jazz shook her head. 'Everything's down. Does anyone know how long this storm will last?'

'If I could get the Internet up, maybe I could tell you. Best guess?' He shrugged. 'It's set in for a while. I shot off an email to Sharif earlier on today to let him know you took a tumble, no harm done. I also reassured him that the women of the village are taking good care of you. I just can't be sure the mail got through before the connection went down.'

'So we're stranded?'

'Looks like it. Nothing's changed for me, Jazz. I work here.'

But everything had changed for Jazz, her eyes behind the veil told him.

Then, remembering who she was and where her duty lay, and that she should not be holding his stare like this, she looked away as the headman began to speak.

'Don't worry, Jazz,' Tyr murmured discreetly. 'I won't let any harm come to you.'

'I can look after myself, Tyr,' she murmured back. 'Storms in the desert are nothing new to me.'

Something told him Jazz wasn't referring to the weather conditions.

By the time things got under way, the searing heat of afternoon had faded to a comfortable warmth, while the sand flurries outside the windows had bathed everything inside the hall in a deceptively muted glow. Tyr gradually edged his way to the back of the crowd, where he could observe without being observed. As expected, there were speeches from several of the village elders, but then a group of old men ushered him forward until he found himself standing next to Jazz at the foot of an improvised stage.

'This won't last long,' Jazz reassured him,

knowing his dislike of being in the spotlight. 'Just a formal vote of thanks for helping out, I think, and then you can leave.'

He hummed, wishing he felt as confident as Jazz. There was an air of anticipation surrounding them that he couldn't account for, and when he glanced around, people smiled back at him as if they were sharing a great piece of news. The villagers' initial shock at Jazz's unconventional arrival at the village in his arms must have faded, he guessed, but was that it?

'I told you things would soon return to normal,' Jazz said confidently.

'I hope you're right,' he replied with less enthusiasm, remembering his bizarre conversation with the headman.

'I am right,' Jazz assured him as the speeches continued on.

He was soon distracted by some alluring scent she was wearing and the seductive rustle of her robe. Jazz was certainly playing the traditional card now, and had dressed for this session in the village hall in a plain black robe with only her expressive eyes on show. Eyes and tiny feet, he noted, telling himself not to be so ridiculous as to be affected by the sight of a set of shell-pink toenails.

'Excuse me.'

Careful not to touch him, she moved past him to stand with the elders who had invited Jazz to join them on the stage. Gesturing for quiet, she began to speak. He couldn't understand every word in Kareshi, but he knew enough to raise his hands in a signal that he had done no more than his job when Jazz praised him and everyone turned to face him and applaud. Then the headman beckoned for him to join Jazz on the stage and the smiling crowd parted for him.

'The headman's just explained that we'll be working together as a team,' Jazz translated, leaning forward as the headman took up his position between them.

Blood rushed to his temples as the headman began to speak, but good manners forced him to remain silent until the old man had finished. He didn't need an interpreter to judge the mood of the crowd. They were jubilant. Some of the men started clapping him on the back. He turned to Jazz, who said something in Kareshi, and the cheers grew louder.

'What did you say?' he demanded, but the headman distracted her and she turned away.

'What did you say?' he repeated when Jazz started waving to the crowd.

Jazz was like a fire burning too bright, in danger of consuming everything around her, including him. What was she keeping from him? It wasn't enough for her to smile and nod her head in his direction, when not once had she held his gaze.

And now the headman stepped forward to speak again.

'If there's something I should know, you'd better tell me now, Jazz,' he warned in an urgent undertone.

Putting a finger over her mouth beneath the veil, Jazz shook her head as the headman cleared his throat and began to speak. He was brandishing a sheet of paper, which Tyr guessed must be an email that had arrived when the Internet was still up. Who could possibly evoke this level of response simply by sending an email? Only one name sprang to mind, and that was his friend Sharif. 'What the hell is going on, Jazz?'

'I'm sure there's nothing to worry about. The headman says it's very good news.'

For whom? he wondered.

'I'm hoping it's a reply to the mail I sent to Sharif, requesting more funding for the school,' Jazz explained.

'So what is he saying now?' he demanded as the headman waved his arms and called for silence. A cold blade of dread sliced through him as Jazz paled and swayed. She looked as if she was about to faint. 'What is it, Jazz? What is he saying?'

'We've got the money for the school.'

'Aren't you happy about that?'

'Of course I am. And the headman has just explained that we will both be staying on to supervise the setting up of the school.'

'Both?' He frowned.

'Tyr—I don't know what to say— Everything's out of control— This is all going too fast—'

'What is?' he demanded.

'The headman just confirmed that Sharif has also agreed to his request that when I do get married it will be here in the village.'

A storm of emotion hit him as cheers rose around them. 'Not to the emir, I hope?'

'Not to the emir,' Jazz confirmed to his relief, but the tears in her eyes did nothing to reassure him.

'Then to whom?' he demanded, the punch in his gut delivering the answer before Jazz had chance to speak.

'The headman's somehow got the idea that I'll be marrying you,' Jazz told him faintly above the roar of the crowd.

CHAPTER NINE

'WE NEED TO TALK, Jazz.'

'We certainly do,' she agreed, all business now, 'but not here and not now. These people deserve everything we can do for them, but the one thing they don't need is our problems on their shoulders.'

The meeting was breaking up. 'We've got work to do. You go and round up the children, while I make sure everyone gets home safely.'

'And then we'll talk,' Jazz assured him tensely.

'You bet we will. I'll come and find you.'

'Tell me you're not thinking of coming round to check out my accommodation?'

'The headman's little speech has changed nothing, Jazz. I still owe it to your brother to keep you safe, so, however much of a pain in the backside you are, that's exactly what I'm going to do.'

'I've lived in the desert all my life, Tyr.'

'In a palace, Jazz.'

'Have you forgotten our camp-outs when we were younger?'

How could he ever forget? Worms in his bed? Stones in his boots?

'Back off, Tyr. Just leave me to work this out, will you?'

'I'd love to,' he assured her, 'but something tells me it's going to take a concerted effort to solve this one. And right now, I have bigger concerns, like making sure you're safe. One thing I do know is that Sharif would never forgive me if any harm came to you. More importantly, I would never forgive myself.'

Straightening up, Jazz pulled the regal card. 'My people will make sure I'm safe. And now, if you will excuse me?'

He almost bowed mockingly, but he was all out of humour and confined himself to watching from the door as Jazz shepherded the children home through swirls of sand until finally she was lost to sight.

By the time he'd delivered the last older person safely home, the storm had the village in its vicious grip. The roar of sand driven at speed by gale-force winds was deafening and his only concern now was for Jazz. Fighting against the power of the wind with one arm over his face and his bandana tied over his nose and mouth, he finally reached the large guest pavilion nestling against the cliff. His feelings lurched from concern to relief when he spotted the hurricane ropes connected to the cliff face, which Jazz had already secured across the entrance.

'Jazz?' Shaking the brass bell, he yelled her name again. He wanted to check the struts holding the pavilion before the wind really got up. 'I'm coming in.'

'Don't let me stop you,' she yelled from somewhere deep inside the tent.

'You should have stayed in the hall until I came back with you to check everything was safe.'

'How many times, Tyr?' Jazz demanded as he closed the roar of the storm out behind him. 'There's no need for you to come and check up on me. Why risk your life for no reason?'

'Maybe I disagree with you about there being no reason for me being here?'

He went about doing the job he'd come for,

shaking poles and checking roof beams. 'Move aside, Jazz. I need to make sure this structure's safe.'

She stalked round after him. 'Do you really think the Wadi people don't know how to build a structure that can weather a storm?'

'Like your brother, Jazz, I have only survived this long because I never take anything for granted.'

'Are you satisfied now?' she demanded, when he stood back to take one last long look around.

'Not nearly,' he said. 'How long do you think you might be confined here? Do you have enough water? Enough to eat?'

'Look around, Tyr.'

He dragged his gaze reluctantly from Jazz to take in the platters set out on low brass tables. They were laden with sweetmeats and fruit. 'Jazz.'

'And don't *Jazz* me. I'm not a child,' she snapped. 'Well? Are you satisfied now? Oh, and there's an underground stream running through the back of the tent, should I start to get thirsty.'

He glared back at her.

'So, what are you going to do now, Tyr? Stroll

back to your place in the village—get knocked off your feet and killed?'

'Hopefully not.' Jazz sounded belligerent, but her expression was both wounded and touchingly concerned for him. This had to be embarrassing for Jazz. According to the headman, they were destined to be married, though not a word of romance had passed between them. Jazz didn't know how to handle it, and for once he had no advice to offer her. 'I'm satisfied you're safe in here,' he said to break the tension.

'The pavilion is well insulated, thanks to its outer skin of camel hide,' Jazz confirmed with a dry throat, clearly relieved to seize the distraction lifeline he'd offered her.

'And you're right, saying no one is safe outside in a storm like this,' he agreed for the sake of encouraging Jazz to use her sensible head, rather than the turbulent emotion he could sense bubbling so close to the surface. 'Not even me.'

'Well, that's something, I suppose.' And then she fell silent. 'You should never have come here,' she said at last in a strained voice.

'I'm supposed to pretend nothing happened

back there?' He jerked his head in the general direction of the village hall.

'Can't you see how bad you're making things look by coming here, Tyr?'

'Your safety comes first. And considering you weren't supposed to be here when I arrived, that's rich, coming from you. But we are where we are, Jazz, and it's no use looking back.'

'If you'd left me on that dune as I asked you to, this wouldn't have happened.'

'If I'd left you on that dune, you'd be dead. And if one of my sisters was stranded in the middle of a sandstorm when Sharif was close by, I would expect him to do exactly what I'm doing for you.'

'But this is different, Tyr.'

'Why? Because you're a princess of Kareshi? You're also a human being, aren't you?'

'I'm alone with a man.'

'Who is here to make sure you're safe, and for no other reason, Jasmina.'

'You can't even call me Jazz now?'

'You're a princess,' he reminded her coldly.

But there was more to it than that. Jazz was the woman he wanted to take to bed, while Princess Jasmina was the innocent sister of his closest friend, and therefore untouchable. Princess Jasmina had nothing to worry about where Tyr Skavanga was concerned. Another tense silence hung between them. And just like the old days, neither one of them was prepared to back down first.

'Well, I might as well be hung for a sheep as for a lamb,' Jazz said finally. 'You're here, and, as you say, we're in this situation, so I might as well offer you a drink.'

He slanted a wry smile at her. 'Charmed, I'm sure.'

'Juice?'

'Thank you.'

While Jazz was arranging things, he took the chance to stare around at all the rich hangings and the jewel-coloured rugs. The Wadi people had really pushed out the boat to show their love for Jazz by offering her the best of everything they had. The smell of precious incense rose from brass burners, while a honeyed light shone from intricately pierced brass lanterns, which were almost certainly centuries old. And there were enough sumptuous throws and hand-sewn silk cushions to make up ten beds.

'It's beautiful, isn't it?' she commented, seeing his interest and perhaps relieved for another chance to move onto safer ground. 'Though you forgot to secure the storm sheet when you came in.'

Surprised, he glanced around.

'You were too busy lecturing me,' Jazz observed dryly as he corrected his mistake.

As he returned and tugged off his jacket, he noticed Jazz staring at him. It occurred to him that in Jazz's ultra-protected world even the flash of a naked biceps would be disturbing. She was staring now at the tattoo that wound around his arm, which was a brutal reminder of his proud Viking heritage and another warning of the many differences between them.

What on earth had persuaded her to allow Tyr Skavanga inside the pavilion? When he'd touched her lightly on the arm with his hand at the meeting, it had felt as if the voltage of the entire national grid had shot through her body. And now she was in lock-down with him? She couldn't allow him to risk his life outside. That was the only reason this was happening, Jazz told herself firmly. But Tyr filled the tent. His aura of power and command surrounded her. He was so brazenly male and so frighteningly virile.

No one could be this close to Tyr and feel nothing, Jazz reasoned sensibly. The ferocity of the storm had unsettled her, but that wasn't an excuse for her imagination to run riot. They were stuck here. They hadn't chosen to be here.

But to be alone with Tyr, when she was never alone with any man apart from her brother? She didn't know where to look, how to act, where to sit.

Look anywhere except at this man mountain, Jazz concluded. *Don't stare at Tyr's hard muscled body covered in scars, and wonder how he came by them. Just accept Tyr for who he is, and what he was when you were both younger and could call him a good friend. Don't stare into Tyr's shadowed eyes and ache to know his past. Don't even begin to think of how it felt when he touched you. Concentrate on practical matters instead, like locking down the pavilion together in preparation for the storm, and everything else will sort itself out.* She hoped.

It was a relief to have something practical to concentrate on, Jazz reflected as she started to move anything breakable out of danger as the wind battered the sides of the pavilion. She was an observer, and a fantasist who had dreamed about Tyr constantly since she was a teen.

But having him here, brutally male and frighteningly close—

'Would you mind if I have a piece of fruit to go with my drink, Jazz?'

Well, that sounded like a threat—not. 'Of course I don't mind. Help yourself.'

Just because Tyr was worldly and she wasn't, it didn't mean he expected anything from her. She'd known him half her life, and Tyr had never done anyone any harm.

Until he became a trained soldier.

Under orders, Jazz reminded herself as she refilled Tyr's goblet and handed it back to him. She blinked when he reached for the dagger at his belt. She remembered exactly when Sharif had given him the dagger. It was the same deadly curving *khanjar* her brother wore hanging from his belt. Sharif had said the gift of a dagger bound Tyr and he as close as brothers, and there was no one in the world he trusted more. As if hypnotised, she watched Tyr slice the fruit into slim pieces with that same lethal blade and put some on a plate to tempt her.

'We could be here for hours, Jazz. You should eat something.'

Hours? One crucial word broke through. How was she going to remain calm and sensible for hours alone with Tyr when her heart was already going crazy?

Jazz accepting the plate of fruit was a turning point. It was a small but significant step towards her relaxing around him. If she couldn't do that, this was going to be a long night for both of them.

'Good?' he prompted as she lifted a sliver of fruit to her lips.

'Thank you.'

She was so prim, so tense, so frightened of him. This was a new Jazz indeed, though her black eyes and perfectly sculpted features had never seemed more beautiful to him.

'Why are you staring at me?' she demanded suspiciously.

'Am I staring?'

'You know you are.'

She blushed and turned away, then moved at the same moment he did for a second piece of fruit. As their arms brushed, she took in a swift gulp of air. The jolt to his own senses stunned him. This was crazy. Sheltering from the storm had become an exercise in restraint he hadn't expected.

Only when Jazz had put half a pavilion's distance between them did she start talking to him again. 'I'm glad you're back, Tyr.'

He stabbed another piece of fruit. 'Glad I'm back from my travels?' he enquired, biting the succulent fruit from the tip of the knife. 'Or glad I'm here?'

'Both,' Jazz admitted frankly, hugging herself tight as the wind threatened to tear the roof off the pavilion.

'So, what do you suggest we do now?'

'What do you mean?' Her eyes widened as she stared at him.

He gave a short laugh, but there was no humour in it. 'Do you tell the emir we spent the night together, or do I?'

'Do you mind if we talk about something else?'

He shrugged as he refilled his goblet with juice. 'Whatever you like.'

He began to pace. Inactivity didn't suit him, but wherever his strides took him in this confined space, it could never be far enough away from Jazz. Wanting her was like a slow burn eating him up inside. 'Why don't we start with your plans for the future?' he suggested.

'My plans?'

He was instantly alert at the touch of steel in Jazz's voice. 'I'm going to continue working at my brother's racing stables, and I'm going to extend my work with our people. My brother has always wanted me to work for Kareshi. Don't look at me like that, Tyr. Sharif has always known where my future lay. It just took me a little longer to see the light.'

'And now you have it all worked out.'

'Men make plans. Women improve them.'

'Was I part of your plan?'

'No,' she exclaimed, sounding genuinely shocked. 'And if you think for one moment that I manufactured this insane wedding idea, you're completely wrong.'

'All right,' he placated her. 'So we know the

people of Kareshi love and respect you, and you are right in saying this is where you belong. I'm just not sure that I do long-term, Jazz.'

She was silent for a moment. 'Do you believe in fate, Tyr?'

He shrugged. 'Where the hell is this leading us, Jazz?'

'Bear with me for a moment, Tyr. It's quite simple. Do you think things happen for a reason? You must do,' Jazz argued before he could say a word. 'Look at the evidence. The fall brought me to Wadi village. The storm kept me here. And now—'

'And now?' he prompted.

'And now, apart from the fact that the events of the past couple of days have woken me up so I can see clearly where my future lies, it's also given me chance to talk to you.'

'What about?' He was in no mood for an inquisition, and barriers had snapped around him before he had even finished asking Jazz the question.

'We're stuck here, Tyr. You've been away a long time. We have lots to talk about.'

Nothing could ever keep Jazz down for long,

he remembered. Jazz Kareshi was as complicated as the politics of her country. She had grown up surrounded by intrigue and danger. Forced to negotiate pitfalls and double-dealing since she'd been a very small child, she knew how to survive pretty much anything; even a surprise wedding announcement, it turned out.

'All right, I'll start,' she said. 'I'm going to live here in Wadi village. At least for the time being.'

'You're going to live here?'

'Why not? I can commute to the stables.'

'What about your home at the palace?'

'What's the point of living in a palace distanced from my people, when I can be here where I can see their problems for myself?'

He couldn't argue with that. 'I don't think Sharif will have any trouble accepting that decision. You know as well as I do that as far as Sharif is concerned, all the pomp and ceremony surrounding his position is just a necessary part of the job. It's the people of Kareshi that matter most to both of you.'

'And I can be quite determined when I put my mind to something.'

'You don't say,' he murmured dryly.

'Where are you going?' Jazz asked as he turned to go.

'Back to my own place. And don't look so worried. I'll make it safely.'

'I'm not worried, but it's your turn now. This is an opportunity for us to catch up, Tyr.'

'I've been here long enough, Jazz. Your reputation is already in tatters.'

'My reputation is shot,' she argued. 'You couldn't have caused more of a sensation if you kissed me in public.'

He paused with his hand on storm cloth over the entrance. 'Now, why didn't I think of that?

'Tyr.'

'Next time I'll leave you where I find you,' he vowed before Jazz could get started.

'No. You'd never do that. You always were the white knight, Tyr.'

Their eyes met and held a dangerous beat too long. 'Not many people would call me that.'

'No,' she agreed, 'they'd call you a hero.'

'Leave it, Jazz—'

'No. I won't leave it.' Her voice was every bit as loud and angry as his. Standing up, all five feet two of her bristling with pent-up frustration, she stood between him and the only way out. 'One day you will tell me why you always avoid talking about the past.'

'My past is none of your business.'

'It is my business,' Jazz said fiercely, 'because, like my brother, I care for you, and I refuse to watch you suffer on your own.'

'Maybe I want to be on my own,' he fired back. 'Believe me, Jazz, you don't want to go where I've been, and you certainly don't want to see what I've seen—not even in your head.'

CHAPTER TEN

IT WAS HIS turn to tense up when Jazz put her hand in his. 'That's where you're wrong,' she said. 'You underestimate me, Tyr. You can tell me anything. *Anything*,' she stressed.

'Some things are best left unsaid, Jazz.'

'I don't agree.' She shook her head and walked away a little distance. 'If you keep all those ugly thoughts inside you they'll just fester until they make you ill. Everything has to be faced at some point, Tyr. Look at me. I've made a mess of things, and now I've got to put them right. I haven't a clue where I'm going to begin with this marriage nonsense, but I'll sort it somehow.' She sighed, but her compassion was all for him. 'I can't pretend to understand the enormity of the memories you're avoiding.'

He said nothing.

'And I can't imagine what you've seen.'

Thank God for that.

Jazz's gaze was unswerving. 'I'm not going to stand by and see a friend in trouble without trying to help.'

'I'm not in trouble.' And he wasn't into spilling the past as Jazz had suggested he should, but as she continued on he had a great sense of the girl he used to know returning, and that was the only news that mattered to him. The strong, practical, sometimes crazy, always feisty, dangerously impulsive girl he used to know was back, while the prim contrivance Jazz had turned herself into in the hope of reassuring one small sector of Kareshi's population that not everything in their country was changing at breakneck speed had been forced to take a back seat. Great.

'And as for that…' She paused and bit her lip.

'Marriage nonsense?' he suggested.

'You might not want to hear this, Tyr, but physical contact between a man and a woman in Kareshi can only mean one thing.'

He refocused on Jazz's concerned face. 'But there's nothing going on between us, so everyone's wrong.'

Jazz shook her head. 'We can't sort this out as easily as that. Whatever we know to be the case, those who would seize on anything in order to destabilise Sharif's peaceful rule will refuse to be convinced. It doesn't suit them. Can't you see that?'

'So, what are you suggesting?'

Taking a deep breath, Jazz braced herself. 'It's too late to save my reputation and I won't risk either of us losing the trust of my people.'

'We know that.'

'So, it's simple,' she said. 'We'll get married, just like the headman said.'

He almost laughed. 'That's insane.'

'No, it isn't,' Jazz argued. 'It's a practical solution. And don't look so horrified. We won't be living as man and wife. There'll be no passion involved. And we can still be friends.'

While he was still absorbing this ill-advised plan, Jazz came up to him and, standing on tiptoe, she brushed her lips against his cheek. 'Friends?' she whispered.

Her touch scorched him. Taking hold of her arms, he moved her back. 'Don't,' he warned.

Needless to say, Jazz refused to be put off. 'I promise I won't tie you down, Tyr. You can leave Kareshi any time you want, and we'll get divorced quietly at some point in the future when all the fuss has died down.'

'Love's young dream?' He shook his head disbelievingly. 'Jazz, you've come up with some madcap plans in the past, but this one is heading for the history books.'

'No, it isn't,' she argued firmly. 'We both trust each other to do what's right, so this is the perfect solution. Don't look at me like that. I have to do something, and this is the best I can come up with. The best for both of us. You don't want to lose the people's trust any more than I do. No one needs to know how we live out our private lives, and this way we can still live in Kareshi and work together.'

Holding up his hands, he stopped her. 'I can't believe you're serious about this.'

'I've never been more serious in my life. Can you think of a better solution?'

'You bet I can. I leave now. And you leave the moment the storm passes over and the helicopter can get here to take you home. You get on with your life, and I get on with mine. Separately.'

'I'm not leaving my people. And as far as we're

concerned, in their eyes the damage is already done.'

'All I can see is you panicking, and proposing to go ahead with some mockery of a ceremony that's supposed to convince your brother, my sisters *and* your people into believing you and I are intending to spend the rest of our lives together. I've backed some of your crazy ideas in the past, Jazz, but this is way beyond reasonable.'

'Tyr. Come back here! Please, listen to me.'

He stared down at Jazz's hand on his arm and she quickly removed it.

'What do you suggest?' Her voice was quiet, but her eyes were direct and unflinching.

He pulled away. 'I don't have to suggest anything. Nothing's changed, as far as I'm concerned. The people of Wadi village accept me for who I am. They always have.' Which was one of the reasons he'd stayed so long. No one asked him any questions.

'But that will change now,' Jazz assured him tensely. 'You will never be able to work here again, because if you don't marry me after spending so much time alone with me, the people you care so much about will shun you.'

'Why would they do that, Jazz?'

'Because in their eyes you will have disgraced their princess.'

With a laugh, he shook his head. 'You make a great case, but I'm not going for it.'

She went rigid. 'A great case? I hope you're not sticking with the idea that I'm trying to trick you into marriage, because nothing could be further from the truth.'

'I just know this crazy idea of yours is going no further. *I* will explain to the people of Wadi village that our relationship is nothing more than a friendship of long standing, and Sharif will understand.'

'If we were in Skavanga, I might agree with you, but this is Kareshi and you have no idea how wrong you are.'

Firming his jaw, he turned away from her. 'This conversation is over, Jazz.'

'Don't you dare,' she warned with all the old spirit. 'Don't you dare mistake me for some spineless pawn who accepts whatever scrap you care to throw at me. I'm trying to do the best I can to repair the damage *I've* done. And, yes, I can stand up for myself and I don't need your help, but you're involved in this whether you like it or not and you can't just walk away. These are my people and you're in danger of offending them, and no one loves these people more than I do. Yes, they're flawed, but so am I. We all are. We're human, Tyr, and flaws come with that territory. No one understands the people of Kareshi better than me. All I'm asking is the chance to continue working with them. I can see now that my idea to marry the emir to strengthen our borders and appease the traditionalists was a terrible mistake, but I'm not going to allow a second terrible mistake to ruin my chances of helping my people.'

'Jazz, you need to sit down and think through things calmly,' he advised, but even he knew it was too late for that.

'I shouldn't have been up there on the dune,' she said, shaking her head. 'If only I'd ridden a different way, none of this would have happened.'

'So don't pile another mistake on top of that one.'

'How fortunate you are to be exempt from the shortcomings that afflict the rest of the human race,' she called after him as he started to unbuckle the storm cloth.

The wind howled in and nearly knocked her over. He reached out to save her and Jazz grabbed hold of his arm. She was pulling at him with all her strength to keep him in the tent, and yelling at him above the ear-splitting howl of the storm. 'Are you mad? You'll be killed out there.'

'So, what do you want me to do, Jazz? Spend the night with the forbidden princess? Will that help your cause? Well?' he demanded, shouting in her face.

Jazz's tears shocked him rigid. He'd done so many things that haunted him, and in the process had changed, or so he had believed, into another, callous and more dangerous person. He was a trained killer, a dangerous man, but right now he was only aware of a pressing need to reach out and help Jazz in every way he could.

'Please don't leave me, Tyr.'

Jazz's voice was small and made the impulse to drag her close unendurable. Her quiet strength reached out to touch some hidden part of him. Relaxing his grip so the cover fell back into place, he secured it firmly, then, taking her hand as if Jazz were a child again, and he the youth who had always looked out for her, he led her back into the heart of the pavilion.

'We will find a solution to this marriage problem,' he promised, wondering for the first time in his life if he could keep his promise to Jazz. He had never let her down before, but this time maybe he would. She'd gone without so much in her young life, compared to the camaraderie he'd enjoyed with his sisters, and then, to all intents and purposes, he'd come along and stolen her brother away. 'I owe you,' he murmured, thinking back.

'More juice?' she suggested, her lips slanting in a small smile.

Her hands were shaking, he noticed, but she clasped them tightly round the goblet in the hope he wouldn't see. He watched her gather herself in a way Jazz used to do as a child. She had always had a backbone of steel.

'I owe you an apology, Tyr,' she stated levelly, not disappointing him. Raising her head, she looked straight at him. 'I got us into this mess and I couldn't regret it more. I just get so frustrated sometimes, and I know I come up with some wild ideas—'

'Wild?' He relaxed. 'You can't go round kissing men and proposing to them.'

Jazz's cheeks flamed red. 'Yes, I know. I feel embarrassed about that. If I'd had my choice you'd have been a long way down the queue.'

He laughed, relieved to see her relaxing at least a little. 'You're a beautiful woman, Jazz. You don't need to do any of that. And I'm not just talking about what the world sees. You're beautiful inside, and you deserve better.'

'Than you?'

'Much better than me. And better than some emir you don't even know. You'll fall in love one day, and when that day comes you won't want baggage. Believe me, I know all about that.'

'You're not married, are you?' Her smile vanished.

'Me? No. The women I meet have got more sense.'

'I think you'd be a good catch,' Jazz argued.

'Do you?' Once again they were staring at each other and all sorts of wicked thoughts were flying through his head, but best of all was the fact that maybe their friendship could move on now.

'Why don't you tell me about the baggage, Tyr?'

It had always been a mistake to relax around Jazz.

She stared at him in silence for a moment. 'It's another of those things you don't want to talk about, isn't it, Tyr?'

He shrugged. 'You've known me most of your life, Jazz, but people change over time.'

'So I'll get to know you all over again.' She met his stare steadily. 'I don't see anything different, Tyr. I just see you. And I'm not afraid of anything you have to tell me, but I think you are.'

'Where are we going with this?'

'If you point-blank refuse to tell me about your past, then all that's left to talk about is you agreeing to marry me.'

She said this lightly as he raked his hair with frustration. 'I thought you'd agreed we would forget that.'

'You're not making this easy for me, Tyr.'

'Easy?' He laughed. 'Nothing about this situation is easy, Jazz.'

She huffed a smile. 'Bet marriage was the last thing on your mind when you heaved me out of that sand drift.'

He slanted her an amused glance. 'You could say.'

'And now if you don't marry me, I will be known to one and all as the disgraced princess of Kareshi. My people will never forgive you for that,' she said, growing serious, 'and neither will Sharif. He might be a forward-thinking leader, but he would never do anything to risk losing the hard-won trust of our people. I'm sorry, Tyr, but there really is no alternative—for either of us.'

'Do you know how mad that sounds?'

'Not mad,' Jazz said sadly, 'realistic. The emir won't have me now, and neither would any other man in our world. I could run away and live somewhere else, I suppose, but I wouldn't be much use to my people.'

For once he was lost for words. Finally, he said tensely, 'Can you hear that?'

Jazz frowned. 'Hear what, Tyr?'

'Exactly.' The wind had dropped. 'The storm

has passed over. People will be on their way round to check up on you very soon and you don't want me here when that happens.'

'It's too late to worry about that, Tyr,' Jazz assured him with a rueful smile.

Freeing the storm sheet, he stepped outside. Unfortunately, Jazz was right. He stopped short on the threshold of the pavilion as a group of villagers came up to him, wanting to know their princess was safe. He saw the exchange of glances when he tried to reassure them, then realised they assumed Jazz was safe because he had been with her throughout the storm. How could he betray these good people? He couldn't indulge his wanderlust any more than Jazz could run away. He was definitely going to stay and see this out.

As he walked away, he could feel the villagers' stares on his back. They weren't hostile—quite the contrary. They seemed delighted by the developing relationship between him and Jazz. There was just one thing wrong with that. He didn't want a wife, and the last person on earth he'd risk sweeping into his dark world was Jazz, though he could still feel the brush of her lips against his cheek, and the softness of her body beneath his hands. He would never forget how she'd trembled when he'd barely touched her, or her delicious scent that wound round his senses. He wanted Jazz in every way that a man could want a woman, but would he be forced into marrying her? That was too crazy to contemplate, and it wasn't going to happen. There had to be a way out of this for both of them. And whatever that way was, he would find it.

CHAPTER ELEVEN

HE SPENT A restless night and was out before dawn the next day. He had to get out and think. He had to drive himself hard until the right idea came to him. The chill of night was still in the air he rode into the echoing canyon. An underground stream surfaced and ran from here to feed the oasis. It deepened into a small lake or wadi, from which the nearby village took its name. This was where he usually stopped to let his horse drink.

Easing back in the saddle, he allowed his mount to pick out a safe path down the steep embankment to the water, where he dismounted. Stretching, he turned to run up his stirrups and make the horse comfortable. Loosening its girth, he secured the reins and gave it an encouraging slap on the neck, though after their fast gallop here his horse needed no encouragement to drink. Stripping off his shirt and jeans, he dived into the icy water. It cleared his mind and soothed him as he worked out where to go from here.

He needed space from Jazz to figure out how to leave without ruining her. It was too late to regret what had happened. He had to find a solution that would work for both of them. Jazz had led a sheltered life, but that hadn't stopped her dreams being big. He could relate to that. Now she was old enough, she was putting those dreams to good use on behalf of her people. He could relate to that too. The sister of his closest friend, a woman he found dangerously attractive, should have been the perfect match for him—would have been perfect, if he hadn't had so many ghosts dogging his footsteps.

He took out his frustration in a powerful freestyle stroke that took him within sight of the dunes at the far end of the wadi. Swimming back, he waded out and shook the water off himself like a wolf. Reaching for his jeans, he tugged them on and shut his eyes, as if that would close out the image of Jazz.

Then his horse whinnied, and, shading his eyes, he saw her riding flat out. He would have known her anywhere. No other woman rode with Jazz's grace and elegance, or with such confidence. Silhouetted against the pale sapphire sky of dawn, with her hair flying loose like a banner, she was leaning low over her horse's neck. He followed her progress with admiration, and then she spotted him. Goodness knew how she knew exactly where he was standing travelling at that speed, but she reined in and rode directly towards him. Something twisted inside him as she approached. Jazz belonged here, just as he did. She was in her element riding free in the desert, but as a deserted wife she would never be free again in Kareshi, at least not free as he understood the term.

He barely had chance to turn around and act nonchalant as she came clattering towards him across the stony ground. Sitting back in the saddle, she smiled at him as she slapped her stallion's neck. 'So I found you.' Kicking her feet out of the stirrups, she jumped down. Having drawn the reins over her stallion's head, she turned to give him one of her slant-mouthed smiles.

'I'll take him,' he offered as her stallion pranced impatiently on the spot.

'No need,' she insisted.

'There is need,' he argued. 'Sometimes even you have to accept help, Jazz.' He took charge of the horse and led both their mounts down to the shallows to drink.

As she battled to rule her veil and put it back in place after her hectic ride, Jazz realised she had hoped she would find Tyr at the wadi. She'd been thinking about him all night. Thinking about his past, and everything Sharif had told her about Tyr's time in the army, which wasn't nearly enough. Sharif had been discreet in the extreme, she suspected, filling in only a few of the gaps for her. Tyr had stayed behind after the conflict to rebuild where he could, but what had happened to him before that? This was her chance to ask him, but somehow as she stared at Tyr's strong back when he took their horses down to the water, the right words refused to form. Perhaps she was afraid of being stone-walled again, because that would be just one more sign of how far they'd grown apart, but she had to set some things straight.

'You would never leave Kareshi because of

what's happened, would you, Tyr? Not when the village needs you.'

'The longer I stay at Wadi village, the more people will talk. If I don't leave, then you should, Jazz.'

'Why should I leave when the damage is already done?'

Catching hold of her arms, Tyr brought her in front of him. 'Will you stop arguing for once?' he demanded, staring fiercely into her eyes.

She was ready for anything, but not that. The touch of Tyr's hands on her body was electrifying. But Tyr felt nothing, Jazz concluded as his stern gaze drilled into hers.

'I'm thinking of you, Jazz. The villagers are getting used to seeing us together and if we stay on they will get carried away by this idea of a marriage between us. If that happens I will have ruined you. As you say, you'll never be able to marry.'

'Do you seriously think I'd want to after this?' She confronted Tyr's stormy gaze with amusement. 'How do you expect me to feel, Tyr? I don't like this any more than you do.'

So the thought of marrying Tyr has never occurred to you?

'I'm still trying to find you a way out of it, Jazz.'

'There is no way out of this.' She stared out across the water. 'Shall we swim the horses while we're here?'

'If you like.'

She exhaled with relief. They had used to swim the horses in the wadi when they were kids. It was a great way to ease tension, and there had never been a better time to reinstate that tradition.

Their horses plunged forward, heading in the direction of a sandbank where they could find solid ground. Once they were safely out of the water, Jazz turned her face to the brightening sky and smiled as she dragged in a lungful of air. Just this one last time, she wanted to escape reality and feast on the innocent pleasures of Kareshi. 'Can you smell the desert, Tyr?'

'Camel dung and heat?'

'You're such a savage. That's Arabian jasmine and desert lavender. The scent is so intense, because our horses' hooves have crushed the flowers.'

'If you say so.'

Romance was clearly the last thing on Tyr's mind this morning. She could hardly blame him, Jazz thought as he sprang down. Preparing to dismount, she held out her hand so Tyr could steady her on the slippery bank, but he bypassed her hand and gripped her round the waist to lower her gently to the ground. The touch of his hands was everything she had ever dreamed of, but the instant her feet were firmly planted, he stepped away. Shading his eyes, he stared across the tranquil water.

'I should be getting back, Jazz.'

'But this is our chance to talk about you. You got away with it last time, but I won't let you get away with it twice.'

He turned to look at her. 'So what do you want to know about me?'

'Everything,' she said softly.

'A princess of Kareshi might be entitled to many things, but those privileges don't extend to me, Jazz.'

'So I'm not allowed to know anything about

the man who used to be my friend. And still is my friend, I hope?'

'I don't know what you want me to say.'

Jazz shrank inside. There was nothing in Tyr's voice for her, nothing at all. She'd tried to reach him and she'd failed. The tiny amount of progress they'd made while they were swimming their horses and relaxing in each other's company had vanished. Closing her eyes, she knew with certainty she didn't want to travel another yard with a man who didn't want her, but she also knew she would never stop trying to reach Tyr, if there was even the smallest chance she could help him.

'Come on, Jazz. Make a decision,' he prompted. 'I've got to get back.'

'I had intended to take a quick look at the caves.'

'Why?'

Because this was her last-ditch attempt to re-establish contact with him. There were prehistoric paintings in the caves, to which, on one memorable occasion, Jazz had added her own childish daub. Sharif had been furious and had ordered her painting removed. Tyr had defended her, insisting Sharif needn't worry as the rainy season would soon see to that. And it had, washing away Jazz's painting, leaving the art of prehistory untouched. They had explored the caves endlessly when they were younger. Maybe revisiting them would light that spark again, she hoped.

'What are you playing at, Jazz?' Tyr called after her as she set off.

'Nothing.' She shrugged as she quickened her stride. 'Just progressing our catch-up plan.'

'*Your* catch-up plan.'

Jazz looked so appealing in pale, figure-hugging riding britches, with the long, concealing shirt she wore over them rippling in the breeze. A flowing dark veil completed the picture, and, whether this was sensible or not, Jazz was the best thing he'd seen since he last saw her the previous night.

'I'm going to ask Sharif if we can open the caves to the public,' she explained, slowing to view the cliff path ahead of them. 'We should share the history of Kareshi. All we'd need to do is to build a proper path with handrails up this cliff and train some guides.'

We, we, we. As Jazz continued to ride her enthusiasm, he wondered if he was guilty of overreacting, or if Jazz still imagined they could live together here? Surely she'd had time to think about it, and had realised what a bad match they were?

It seemed not, and as Jazz started up the cliff, he brushed away a twist of unease and followed her.

'Be careful when you come up here, Tyr. This scree is treacherous.'

'Jazz!'

His heart stopped as she wobbled precariously on the edge of a narrow ledge. Bounding up, he dragged her to safety, and for a few intense moments they just stared at each other, and then, conscious he was still holding on to her, he lifted his hands away.

'Don't make such a fuss, Tyr.' Jazz was straightening her shirt as she spoke. 'I know this terrain like the back of my hand.'

'Terrain changes over time, and just as sand can slip away beneath your horse's hooves, these small loose stones are deadly underfoot. You could have gone over the edge.'

'But I trust you to save me.'

He flinched as she touched his arm. 'Then you're mad.' He turned away before the urge to unloop Jazz's veil and kiss the life out of her overwhelmed him.

And that was all they had time for before Jazz's riding boot hit a patch of loose stones and she started to slide away from him. Yanking her back, he stared into the face of a woman he wanted, a woman who, judging by the look on her face, badly wanted to be kissed. He didn't need any encouragement. Removing her veil, he looped it around her neck and drew her close. Her breathing quickened and her lips parted. 'What are you doing?' she whispered.

His answer was to dip his head and brush his lips against hers. Jazz responded as he'd hoped she would, melting against him as she reached up to link her hands behind his neck. He pulled away, cursing himself for the loss of control when he felt her trembling. 'And now we really should be getting back.'

'You're right,' she agreed, swallowing deep. 'Do you mind if I take hold of your hand for the rest of the way down?'

'Be my guest.'

By the time they reached level ground, reason had thankfully re-entered his thinking. 'You're going to ride into the village ahead of me.'

A frisson of concern tore through Jazz. The tone of Tyr's voice had changed so completely. He'd kissed her. Tyr had kissed her. But in the short time it had taken them to walk down the cliff path together, he had grown distant again. The fact that Tyr could cut himself off so completely, and in so short a space of time, frightened her. There was so much she didn't know about him, and it distressed her to think things were so messed up between them she was in real danger of losing the friendship of a man she had loved since she was a child.

As they mounted up in silence, Jazz reflected that if the past few weeks had taught her anything, it was that she couldn't write the script for a perfect life, because everyone had different aspirations. Tyr's dream was to rebuild, then move on to the next project, while hers was to stay and develop what she started. His kiss had been a fleeting reminder of what might have been, but Tyr obviously thought the kiss was a mistake.

The time she'd spent with him had been an unexpected gift, but it was over now. Urging her mount into a brisk trot, she watched Tyr turn his horse around and head in the opposite direction as he took the long way back to the village.

Disbelief racked Tyr. He'd kissed Jazz? What the hell was he thinking? He'd been back at the village for just under an hour when she came to tell him the news. She found him at the village hall, where he was fine-tuning the Internet connection, which he'd managed to get back up.

'I thought you should know,' she said.

'That's putting it mildly. Why don't you start at the beginning and tell me everything in Sharif's mail.'

'You know what email's like. You write one thing and the person at the other end reads something else. I mailed Sharif to explain that we can sort this mix-up out between us, but what I didn't know was that the headman had already mailed Sharif to tell him how happy everyone is at the prospect of us staying on here, once we are married. Please don't be angry, Tyr. This is just a terrible misunderstanding.'

'This is like a sandstorm from hell,' he argued.

Closing down the computer, he steered Jazz outside. The time for worrying what people thought when they saw them together was long past, but Jazz was right in saying it was too late for recriminations. 'When is this ridiculous ceremony supposed to take place?'

'Tomorrow.'

'What?'

'I'm sorry, Tyr, but there's no such thing as a long engagement here.'

His face turned thunderous. 'No kidding.'

Tyr had every right to be angry, Jazz conceded as he marched her down the dusty village street towards her pavilion. He left her at the door without a backward glance. He was mad and she didn't blame him. There was no way out of this now, for either of them, unless Tyr was prepared to risk his friendship with Sharif, and she doubted he would ever risk that. She had hoped for enough time to plan a way forward together, but there was no time, and now they were further apart than they had ever been, which meant she was faced by the bitter prospect of a loveless marriage to a friend she'd lost for ever.

No! No! No! His mind was splintering into a thousand pieces, all of them emblazoned with the same word: No. Did he want this sham marriage? Did he want to deceive the people he'd come to care for in Kareshi? Did he want to subject Jazz to a farce on a grand scale? No again. Jazz was innocent, and the people of Wadi village were only guilty of wanting to share their princess's happiness. Having a princess of Kareshi marry in their village was a dream come true for them. How could he walk away from that? And now he'd spoken to Sharif he had confirmation that if he walked away from this, Jazz would never be able to lift her head in Kareshi again. He had to give Sharif credit for remaining strictly neutral throughout a very difficult conversation: 'You're my friend and Jazz is my sister,' Sharif had said. 'I trust you to work this out between you.'

He didn't sleep that night. How could he sleep with Jazz lying half naked in a bed close by? Jazz with her storm cloud of jet-black hair drifting round her shoulders and that sweet mouth begging to be kissed.

He should never have kissed her. He should have stayed away from her.

It was too late to worry about that now. Staring into the darkness, he thought about the irony of Sharif finishing their conversation by begging him to be kind to Jazz when he didn't know any other way to be with her. But Sharif had only seen him at his most brutal recently, Tyr reflected. They might call him a hero and pin a medal on his chest, but he could never imagine bringing new life into such a violent world, and Jazz deserved children.

Swinging out of bed, he paced the floor. Who was he to ruin Jazz's life? He had asked Sharif this same question, only to have Sharif insist that marriage to Jazz might turn out to be the best thing that had ever happened to him, if Tyr would give it only half a chance. But he couldn't bear to see the hurt in her eyes when Jazz finally understood how easy it was for him to close off from all human emotion. And if he were ever selfish enough to wrap his arms around her, he would never let her go. Right now he'd settled for the easy friendship they used to share, though it seemed to him that any type of relationship with Jazz beyond a formal contract of marriage had finally slipped out of his grasp.

* * *

In spite of all her misgivings, Jazz couldn't help but be touched by the amount of effort the villagers were putting into making her wedding day special. She was hyperventilating most of the time at the thought of becoming Tyr's bride. It was amazing how she could cut out all the bits about this being a forced wedding and just think about being married to Tyr. Not that this fantasy version of events was something she could share with him. Fortunately, she didn't have to, as Tyr was careful to keep his distance. There wasn't much time before Sharif arrived to give his blessing, so everyone was rushing to put everything in place.

There was just one spoiler. As she toyed with a veil of the finest Chantilly lace, Jazz shivered as she thought about her wedding night with Tyr.

And Tyr? How must he be feeling?

Probably repulsed at the thought of sleeping with her?

She would almost prefer that, Jazz realised. It would lift her most pressing concern away: *the wedding night.* Perhaps they could come to some sort of mutual arrangement. Separate beds? Sleeping with a friend was totally weird by any standards. Surely Tyr would agree with that? She had a total blind spot when it came to sex. She didn't have a clue, except for what she'd read or overheard. Vowing to remain chaste until marriage hadn't been too big a sacrifice when she only had hair-raising gossip about *the wedding night* to go on. She'd always been chaste and had had no plans to change the status quo.

Until now.

Putting the veil aside before she ruined it, she took a deep breath. *Calm down!* If she carried on like this she would be a gibbering wreck by the time she stood beside Tyr at the ceremony.

Would he even turn up?

The thought that he might not chilled her. The thought that he would led immediately back to their wedding night. She had to try to concentrate on the fact that Sharif and Tyr's sisters and their husbands would be arriving soon, or she would never be able to go through with this. Sharif had delivered his itinerary in one of his customarily brusque texts:

Prepare for full contingent of family members arriving to celebrate with Wadi villagers tomorrow night.

Sharif hadn't mentioned celebrating with his sister. Jazz gathered that Sharif had nothing to say to her of a celebratory nature. And who could blame him? She'd pressed for marriage negotiations with the Emir of Qadar and then she'd changed her mind, only to hit him with the bombshell that she was going to marry Tyr Skavanga. All in all, Sharif was being quite restrained.

For now.

CHAPTER TWELVE

JAZZ WAS OUT of bed at dawn and pacing restlessly. Her wedding day. Her marriage to Tyr! She couldn't believe it. She wasn't sure she wanted to believe it. Britt had texted to confirm the Skavanga sisters were on their way, so that was a relief at least. Having the Skavanga sisters onside equalled having the best support team ever in her corner. She had nothing to worry about, Jazz told herself firmly.

Except her wedding night tonight with Tyr.

Tonight was a long way off.

And Sharif?

She wasn't going to think about her brother now.

And if Tyr didn't turn up?

What if he left her to stew with all the wedding arrangements made and her family arriving? How many people would she let down then? And her heart would break. She loved Tyr. She had always loved Tyr, and even if this wedding was a sham, she was as excited at the prospect as any bride. She could weave a thousand fantasies about marrying Tyr Skavanga, but nothing could compare with the real thing, just so long as she didn't think too much about the future. But would he turn up? Tyr was an adventurer by nature, always seeking the next horizon. Maybe he'd already left Kareshi. Tyr was loyal to her brother, but he was his own man—and, as Tyr had said, did she really know him now? The days of reading him easily were long gone.

The women of the village distracted her from her mixed-up thoughts. She could hear them gathering outside the pavilion, waiting impatiently for the moment when she invited them in so they could prepare her for her wedding day. It was hard not to be swept away by their enthusiasm as they crowded into the pavilion.

She could do this! So long as she stuck to her original plan to ask nothing of Tyr.

But what would he ask of her?

Apprehension fluttered through Jazz at the thought that whatever Tyr expected on their wedding night, she could only disappoint him.

But when she tried to imagine Tyr touching her, Tyr's hands on her body, Tyr, the master of pleasure…

Something of this excitement must have shown on her flushed face. The women had started giggling behind their hands, as if they knew what she was thinking. It was a relief to submit to the beauty treatments they had prepared for her and hope they would soon drop the subject, but it wasn't long before they returned to their favourite topic.

'But it won't be a proper wedding night,' Jazz was horrified to hear herself blurt out.

'Who says it won't be a proper wedding night?'

'Britt!'

Leaping off the cushions, she threw her arms around all three Skavanga sisters as they moved in for a group hug. Now she felt better. And worse. Better because three women she was coming to love had arrived, and worse because she hated deceiving them.

'Why are you crying?' Eva demanded in her no-nonsense way. 'Do you want red, puffy eyes? This is supposed to be a happy time.' This was followed by a big sigh and worried glances Eva exchanged with her sisters.

If her eyes weren't puffy before, they were now. Jazz bit back a laugh as Eva mopped her face vigorously with the sleeve of her rough cambric shirt.

'Enough!' Leila winked at Jazz. 'We're not here to administer exfoliation. We're here to act as cheerleaders for the bride.'

Having nudged Eva out of the way, Leila put her arm around Jazz's shoulders. 'Everyone gets emotional on their wedding day, and we couldn't be happier that you are taking our brother off our hands. So don't worry about it, because we're all here to help.'

But nothing got past Tyr's oldest sister. Britt was staring at Jazz with concern, having sensed in a nanosecond that all was not well with the blushing bride, though to her credit, Britt kept those thoughts to herself.

The sun was already blazing like a merciless brand in a cloudless blue sky as they got down to some serious wedding preparations. Why did time pass so quickly when you wanted it to drag? She wanted this. She didn't want this. She was far too tense to enjoy the moment. She longed to confess everything to Tyr's sisters and seek advice, but she could hardly do that. She couldn't even be certain that she hadn't driven Tyr away again. And how would his sisters feel about that, when they'd only just got him back?

They would never forgive her, and she would never forgive herself.

'So, you're nervous about the wedding night?'

'Eva, do you have to be so blunt?' Leila reprimanded her.

'Yes, I think I do,' Eva insisted, circling Jazz like a mother hen.

Jazz blenched at the thought of revealing her ignorance where matters between a man and a woman were concerned to the three Skavanga sisters, but the women of the village had left the tent to bring Jazz the precious wedding jewels they wanted her to wear, so there was nothing to stop Eva continuing her interrogation.

'It's a simple question.' Eva paused. 'I take it from your public announcement that you're still a virgin, Jazz?'

'And what a question.' Leila showed her outrage on Jazz's behalf. 'Jazz, you don't have to answer that.'

Jazz forced a confident smile. 'Don't worry. I'm not going to.' She added a laugh. But Eva was right. She was scared out of her skin. She didn't have any sexual experience, and, with only old wives' tales to go on, her expectations were hardly encouraging. So here was her dilemma: if Tyr did turn up, she would be afraid of the thought of their wedding night. If he didn't turn up, it would be an unmitigated disaster all round, as well as a tragedy for his sisters, who had only just got used to having him around again. And she would be the cause of that disaster.

'Well, she either is a virgin or she isn't,' Eva insisted stubbornly, without the slightest hint of remorse as she helped herself to a giant-sized lump of honeyed halva. 'There is no in-between. And if the answer's yes, then all I'm saying is that I'm prepared to offer a few useful tips.'

Britt responded calmly. 'Thank you for that insightful comment, Eva, but I really don't think this is the moment for a session of your helpful hints.'

'Eva, can't you remember how you begged us for peace and quiet on your wedding day?' Leila asked. 'Don't you remember how hard it is to remain calm while everyone's adding their own piece of advice? If you must pace up and down the tent munching and scowling, why don't you at least make yourself useful? You could go and find the henna lady to find out how long she's going to be.'

Eva's face fell and she stopped pacing immediately. 'Jazz, I'm sorry. I wasn't thinking.'

Leaping up, Jazz gave Eva a hug. How she longed to ask Eva for some much-needed help so she could get through the ordeal of the marriage night ahead of her, but how could she admit to being a virgin, let alone explain that she was likely to remain a virgin long after tonight?

'I'll go with Eva to help find the henna lady,' Leila offered tactfully, sensing Britt would like some time alone with Jazz.

The moment the cover was over the entrance, Britt asked Jazz the one question she'd been dreading. 'What's wrong, Jazz? Can you tell me?'

Jazz heaved a long sigh. It was so tempting to

tell Britt everything. She had often longed for a sister to confide in, but Britt ran a company and had Sharif to consider. Did Britt need anything else to worry about? 'It's nothing. Just pre-wedding nerves.'

'Well, they're understandable,' Britt agreed, and then she smiled. 'I saw the connection between you two at the party, so I'm not really surprised. But I have to admit I didn't see this coming. Not so fast, anyway.'

No wonder! 'Neither did I,' Jazz admitted truthfully, feeling ten times worse at having to hold things back from Britt.

'I hate to think of you having an accident, but if that tumble from your horse got you two together, it certainly saved a lot of time.' Britt laughed, and then grew serious again. 'If anyone can get my brother to stay in one place, it's you, Jazz. So thank you. I really mean that. And, if it helps, I think you two were made for each other.'

'Do you?'

'Yes,' Britt insisted. 'Fate clearly brought you two together.'

How temptingly close that fantasy version of events seemed now.

'Where is Tyr? Have you seen him?' The anxious words spilled out of Jazz's mouth before she could stop them.

Britt reassured her with a smile. 'Don't look so worried. Tyr's riding with Sharif. The way you look, anyone would think you expect him to leave you standing at the altar.'

I couldn't blame him, Jazz thought as she forced a laugh. 'Was he in a good mood?' She asked the question casually.

'What do you think?' Britt arched a brow.

Good question.

If Tyr and Sharif were riding together, they must be concocting some sort of plan to get Tyr out of this, Jazz concluded.

'Jazz?'

Hearing the note of concern in Britt's voice, she refocused. 'Wedding nerves. I must stop fretting.'

'Indeed you must,' Britt agreed, throwing a thoughtful look her way.

Could it possibly have been a more beautiful evening? Jazz wondered as she stood outside the pavilion with Britt, waiting for everyone to return. The great bowl of the sky provided a violet backdrop for the moon, which was hanging like an ivory swing suspended on moonbeams surrounded by stars. Lifting her face, she closed her eyes and told herself she was going to marry Tyr Skavanga. Now, if that wasn't the stuff of dreams—

Except this had the potential to turn into a nightmare.

An hour or so later, and the wedding party with Jazz at the head of it was ready to leave the pavilion. The front entrance had been opened up, and a vast, jostling crowd had gathered outside to throw petals that had been brought all the way from Skavanga in Jazz's path. Nothing about this celebration smacked of a rushed wedding. Quite the contrary. Thanks to the hard work of Britt, Eva and Leila, together with all the women of the village, she was going to have the fairy-tale wedding she'd always dreamed of, and one Jazz guessed would be remembered for generations to come in Wadi village.

Lifting the hem of her floating chiffon skirt, she could hardly believe she was on her way to marry Tyr. Her heart was singing even if her hands were trembling. She led the way out of the pavilion, followed by Britt, Eva and Leila, who were acting as her bridesmaids. She whispered her thanks as Britt pressed a bouquet of Arctic roses into her hands. She wanted to tell all three of Tyr's sisters that she couldn't remember a time when she hadn't loved their brother, but she couldn't say something that would paint a false picture of this wedding. She had never been more grateful for a veil to hide her mixed and tumultuous feelings. Secured with a glittering diamond tiara studded with the now famous blue-white diamonds mined exclusively at the Skavanga diamond mine, her veil was a fall of Chantilly lace, sprinkled with diamonds and seed pearls that flashed in the light of a thousand torches as she walked along the sandy path to the man she had loved all her life.

'I've never seen anything more beautiful,' Leila said as she walked behind Jazz.

'Don't worry. We'll deduct the cost from Tyr's next dividend,' Eva joked. 'Why are you shivering, Jazz?' Eva added, catching up with Jazz. 'You're not sickening for something, are you?'

Lovesick? Heartsick? Any one of those would do. 'I'm just not used to such a fuss,' she fudged.

'Then you should be,' Eva insisted. 'You're a princess, after all.'

'Every bride's a princess on her wedding day,' Leila agreed.

Jazz shivered again as she touched the cold white stones in her tiara with her fingertips. 'But here's one bride who doesn't deserve all this attention.'

'Of course you do,' Eva insisted. 'Every bride deserves a fuss on her wedding day. And you can always give the tiara back when you're finished with it,' Eva joked. 'In fact, you can give it to me.'

'For goodness' sake, Eva, will you stop teasing Jazz?' Leila cautioned as she came up on Jazz's other side. 'Can't you see she's not in the mood?'

The crowd fell back as they sat Jazz on a camel that had been specially shampooed for the occasion. It was caparisoned with handwoven wedding finery, heavily embroidered with silver thread and tinkling bells, and its swaying gait would announce Jazz's arrival long before Tyr could see her. A collective sigh rippled through the waiting crowd as Jazz drew close to the wedding arbour, which had been decorated with colourful desert flowers. Some of the villagers had climbed up the palm trees to catch a better view of her, and she waved and smiled to them, wishing she could live out their fantasies for her with Tyr.

Tyr. Surely he'd turned up, or someone would have stopped the wedding procession, wouldn't they?

Her gaze found him immediately and relief flooded through her, swiftly followed by the most excitement yet. Dressed in a plain white robe that outlined his impressive frame, Tyr was the only person not looking at her when she arrived. He didn't even glance her way when the boy leading her camel gave it the instruction to kneel, and then helped her to dismount. Perhaps Tyr had persuaded himself that if he didn't look at her, he could preserve the illusion that this was just a bad dream.

And then he turned and it was as if the air had been sucked from her lungs. The look he gave her was devastating. She could almost convince herself that Tyr really did want to marry her.

A great roar rose from the crowd as Sharif

left Tyr's side to escort Jazz under the wedding arbour.

'Brother.' Dipping into a low curtsy brought on another loud cheer.

'You look very beautiful, Jasmina,' Sharif commented as he brought her to her feet in front of him.

Jazz met her brother's keen stare steadily. Everything was going to be all right. She had to believe that, though she couldn't help wondering what the two men had been discussing during their ride. It was too late to ask Sharif now, and she could only be grateful to Britt for smiling reassurance at her as Sharif gave Jazz's hand into Tyr's keeping.

CHAPTER THIRTEEN

SOMETHING HAPPENED WHILE she was standing beneath the wedding arbour alongside Tyr. The turmoil inside her settled and she was filled with a deep sense of calm. Tyr was so strong and true, it was hard not to react that way to him. And he was as passionate and as committed to Kareshi as she was. And though he hadn't wanted this marriage, she had been a fool to doubt he would turn up. Tyr would never flinch from duty any more than she would.

But forget duty. She loved him. She loved Tyr with all her heart, Jazz thought as she stared up at the magnificent Viking at her side. She had always loved Tyr and she always would.

'Do you take this man...?'

'Yes.' Her answer was unhesitating.

'Do you take this woman...?'

'I do.'

Tyr's voice was firm and low and measured.

It was the type of voice that inspired confidence. And it did, inside her. Was she fooling herself? She hoped not, for, against all the odds, she sensed they both knew that what they were doing was right.

Loveless, maybe, but right, Jazz told herself as the formal part of the ceremony drew to a respectful close, and Tyr, who was now her husband, led her carefully down the steps.

Could anything be more romantic? If the night sky had been magical, surely the setting for their wedding feast could not have been more beautiful? The temperature was perfect with just the slightest breeze to play with Jazz's veil. She was seated alongside Tyr on a bank of silken cushions arranged on a priceless rug. They were seated well apart in accordance with tradition, and they hadn't spoken a word to each other since exchanging their vows. This was the expected behaviour of a new bride and groom in Kareshi, but Tyr had certainly taken to the detachment with ease. He was unemotional to a fault, his expression composed, but distant. Until he turned to her and her stomach lurched.

'Would you care for some fruit, or some Arabian coffee?'

She tried to detect some warmth in his voice, but it was the same neutral tone Tyr had used throughout the wedding ceremony. Theirs was a marriage of convenience, Jazz reminded herself, every bit as much as any marriage she might have made to a stranger. She accepted fruit and coffee, knowing she'd taste neither. A young boy stood beside her, waiting to peel the fruit for the bride, should she wish him to, but neither he nor Tyr spoke another word to her, not even when she thanked the boy for filling her jewelled goblet with juice.

She was invisible. She should have been used to this public treatment of a royal princess of Kareshi, but her country's traditions had never seemed quite so draconian before. Because she had dreamed of laughter and intimate glances on her wedding day, secret smiles and potent stares connecting. She'd been to weddings where the fingertips of the bride and groom had touched briefly. Accidentally on purpose, Jazz had always thought, and the air around the newly married couple had sizzled with expectation and suppressed passion. That was what she had dreamed of for her wedding day.

Was it a dream too far? she wondered, risking a glance at Tyr. For all the attention this groom was paying his bride, she might as well have married the Emir of Qadar.

No!

This was nothing like marrying the Emir of Qadar. If she'd married the emir, she would only ever have been able to look at Kareshi over her shoulder. This was infinitely preferable to that. And Tyr was a prince in every respect. Tyr inspired people. Tyr got things done. Tyr was the love of her life. If only this could have been the fairy-tale wedding of her dreams, they might have accomplished so much together.

This was not a fairy-tale wedding and she would not deceive herself into believing it was. She hated deceiving everyone else, for as lovely as they'd made this evening for her, she couldn't wait for it to end so she could be alone with Tyr, and they could sort this out.

Alone with Tyr?

Jazz's mouth dried at the prospect as she glanced at the mountain of muscle beside her.

Did she really want to be alone with Tyr? *Alone in bed with him?*

Alone in bed with both of them naked?

'Did you say something?'

She looked up as Tyr spoke. Her cheeks flamed with heat when she realised that she must have exclaimed out loud with apprehension.

'No. Nothing.'

She pinned a small smile to her face to reassure him. How could she admit that she was terrified at the thought of being alone with him when they'd known each other all their lives?

Anxiously, she began to twist the simple platinum wedding band Tyr had placed on her finger. How disappointing he would find her. Tyr was so vital and masculine, while she knew nothing about physical love between a man and a woman. She had hoped the first time would be special, and not painful, as she'd been told it could be, but beyond that—

'Do you like it?'

'I'm sorry?'

'The ring?' Tyr prompted. 'Do you like it?'

Her eyes must have been wide with dread, Jazz realised. 'I love it.' This was the truth. She loved the simplicity of the Scandinavian design. If she had chosen it herself she couldn't have picked a ring she liked better. But it was sad to think that the ring wasn't a love token, but only the ink to seal the deal. 'How did you find such a lovely ring at such short notice?'

'Britt bought it for me.'

Of course. Tyr would have contacted Britt, who had chosen something she thought Jazz would like. The thought of Britt doing that for her made Jazz feel emotional. She didn't deserve such good people in her life, and she longed to tell Britt the truth.

Tyr stopped her with his hand on her arm as she started to get up to go and find his sister. 'Where are you going?'

'To speak to Britt. I have to explain that this wedding is a sham.'

'You'll do nothing of the sort.' Tyr's voice was low, but insistent. 'Not unless you want to upset everyone who's come here to wish us well.'

'That's the last thing I want, but—'

'Not now, Jazz,' Tyr murmured as the speeches began.

Tyr didn't ask her to translate for him. He'd

heard enough, Jazz guessed. There was no eye contact between them, no contact between them at all. Would things improve when they were alone?

'Are you cold?' he asked as she shivered with apprehension.

Before she could answer, Tyr had draped a cashmere blanket round her shoulders, making her remember times when he would have laughed and dragged her into a wholly innocent bear hug to warm her up.

'Cold and tired?' he diagnosed when she heaved a sigh.

'No.' She would be awake all night, pacing the pavilion.

When they finally got up to leave, Jazz felt like a prisoner walking to her doom, rather than a bride eagerly walking at the side of her husband to her marriage bed. The wedding procession took its time to wind its way with some ceremony around the village before it turned in the direction of the bridal accommodation that had been set aside for them on the banks of the oasis.

The wedding pavilion was very grand and had been erected a tactful distance away from the village. When they walked inside, Jazz gasped to see such luxury. Everything had been provided for the comfort of the bride and groom. There was an abundance of fresh food laid out on platters along with jugs of juice and fresh water. There was also the most enormous bed, which she had to try very hard not to look at.

Next there was a ceremony that allowed Tyr and Jazz to thank everyone for such a wonderful day. She could tell Sharif was slightly embarrassed when it came to his turn, while Britt's hug lasted longest of all. 'You'll be all right,' Britt whispered. 'I know Tyr will take good care of you.'

That was what she was afraid of, Jazz realised as she forced her lips into a smile. 'Of course I'll be all right,' she agreed brightly, with absolutely no evidence to back that up. When everyone had left, the two of them remained standing, staring at each other from opposite sides of the pavilion. There would be entertainment for their guests, Jazz registered numbly as the sound of traditional music floated towards them on the balmy air.

This was no way to get her new life started.

She gathered her courage. 'Would you like to bathe first, or shall I?'

'Why don't you go first?' Tyr suggested. 'Would you like me to help you with your gown?'

'No, thank you.'

They both sounded so stiff. They were as remote as two strangers who had been thrown together for the night.

'No, please—I insist,' she said, putting off the moment when she would emerge from behind the curtain a virgin bride. 'I'm happy to wait while you bathe first.'

All night if necessary.

It was a relief when Tyr disappeared into the curtained section of the tent. This was as far from her fantasy wedding night as it was possible to get, Jazz reflected as she paced nervously up and down, waiting for him to return.

When he did come back, Tyr was covered by only a small towel, which he had secured around his waist. She had to remind herself that where Tyr came from same-sex saunas, followed by rolling naked in the snow, was considered a harmless family activity, rather than some intriguing erotic ritual, so walking about half naked in front of her was nothing new for Tyr Skavanga.

She flashed a smile that didn't quite reach her eyes as Tyr held the curtain leading into the bathing tent for her. This was going to be the longest bathing session in the history of the mountain stream. And now, because she'd been so stubborn in refusing his help, it was going to take her an age to undress. Finally, after much tugging and pulling, she stood naked in the balmy warmth, and, taking the plunge into the stream, she was glad of the shock of the icy water hitting her overheated skin.

'Are you all right in there?' Tyr called out as she exclaimed with shock.

'I'm fine,' she yelled back, sinking low in the water in case he should decide to come and investigate.

Climbing out only when she was in danger of turning into a prune, she grabbed an all-concealing bath sheet and wrapped herself in it like a mummy.

Viewing the various pots of creams and lotions that the women had left for her, Jazz huffed a humourless laugh. The fabled potions of Wadi village were lost on her. These were said not just to smooth the skin but to heighten sensation everywhere they touched. She'd need an industrial bucketful, and a man who showed some interest in applying it.

She took her time to select a nightgown. This wasn't as easy as it sounded, as all the garments the women had left for her seemed to be composed of gossamer-fine silk, and she could see through them quite easily. How was she supposed to face Tyr dressed like that?

This is your one and only chance at marriage. Just for once, can't you allow yourself to want something for you?

Like what? Jazz argued with her inner critic.

Like Tyr making love to you, before your life becomes one of practical solitude.

Allow Tyr to make love to her? He'd have to teach her about sex first.

Why don't you ask him to do just that?

Ask Tyr to teach her about sex? Her cheeks were on fire with embarrassment at that thought. Reaching for a robe, she wrapped it around the flimsy nightgown she had chosen to wear. If Tyr would settle for friendship, then so would she.

No, she wouldn't.

Yes, she would. She might have to.

There was only one way to find out.

She paused and took a deep breath. Her hand was trembling as she gripped the dividing curtain. She had to do this. *She could do this.* She would find a way to reach Tyr and restore communication between them, to clear the air. And then they could talk into the night until they were both so tired they fell asleep.

Coward.

Tyr had made himself comfortable on a bed of cushions as far away from the main bed as possible, Jazz noticed when she returned to the main part of the pavilion. He was resting back with his eyes closed.

Good. Maybe he was asleep.

He closed his eyes as Jazz walked deeper into the pavilion, but he'd seen enough to know she took his breath away. Standing with her back to him, she had begun to brush her hair. The light was behind her, and even though she had thrown a robe over her diaphanous nightgown, he could see her naked form quite clearly. She was easily the most beautiful woman he'd ever seen. As she continued to brush her long, damp hair in smooth, hypnotic strokes, he realised that Jazz had no idea she possessed a magic strong enough to arouse a man who had believed for years he was dead to all but the most primitive feelings. He was painfully aroused now, and emotionally aroused, and all thanks to Jazz Kareshi.

Jazz Skavanga, Tyr amended, smiling to himself as he considered this most surprising of all the recent developments.

Jazz had applied some attractive scent, and the robe she had donned was of some flimsy material in softest coral that picked out the blush in her cheeks. And she was plaiting her hair—

Don't do that. Don't plait your hair. Don't tie it back.

He smiled as he imagined Jazz's reaction to his newfound feelings, but meanwhile frustration was threatening to throttle him. What he needed was another dousing in the freezing-cold stream.

He turned away, feigning sleep as Jazz stood up and turned around to face him. If she had any sense she would go straight to the big marital bed, and then tuck herself in and go straight to sleep. At the very least, she should stay well away from him. He was curious as to what she would do. He'd hunted her down at the party and had wanted her ever since. When she'd fallen from the horse, his heart had stopped beating, and when he'd checked her over for injury, his life had stopped too. He wanted Jazz more than ever now, but though the world might assume he had carte blanche to seduce the woman who was now his wife, Jazz meant more to him that that, and he would never mislead her by promising more than he could deliver.

He breathed a sigh of relief when she turned for the big bed. But would that help him? Having Jazz a few feet away when he had spent most of the wedding ceremony trying to avoid contact with her because the ache of wanting her was so acute? Did he seriously think he was going to make it through the night?

CHAPTER FOURTEEN

IF ACTIONS SPOKE louder than words, then Jazz had no option but to do this. With the prospect of a loveless wedding night ahead of her, what did she have to lose? She stared at Tyr's big, muscular back clad in a black tee. He was wearing black boxers too. She'd sneaked a look.

What a modest bridegroom. What a shameless bride.

When fantasy clashed with reality, all she could think about was Tyr looming over her, magnificent and immense. But if he moved a muscle, she'd probably run a mile.

So was their friendship dead too? Jazz wondered as Tyr remained motionless with his back turned to her. As he continued to ignore her, she wondered if Tyr ever ached for a touch, or a kind word and a warm look, as she did right now. She understood why he'd become hard and self-reliant, but she wanted him to know that she cared, and that this was their wedding night—which terrified her, and challenged her to be more courageous too. Or else, was she doomed to an empty life with a head full of Tyr Skavanga? She gazed at the big, silent Viking, currently stretched out on his bed of cushions just a few yards away. Maybe she should have married the Emir of Qadar.

How lucky was she to have so many choices?

'Jazz?' Tyr murmured her name without opening his eyes. 'Jazz, what are you doing? What the hell!'

'What does it look as if I'm doing?' Having climbed beneath his covers, she pulled them up to her chin. 'I was cold, so I'm joining my husband for our wedding night. The least we can do is share our body heat.'

'No, we can't,' Tyr assured her, putting space between them.

He had tried not to look at Jazz in her diaphanous robe, with her hair streaming round her shoulders, and had failed miserably. The urge to make love to her was overwhelming him. She was lying in his bed, for goodness' sake!

'You'll be more comfortable in the big bed.'

He spoke gruffly, closing his mind to a sight that had cracked his heart wide open *and* left him with the worst case of frustration known to man.

'I might be as comfortable in the big bed, but I wouldn't be as warm,' Jazz argued in a voice he'd never heard her use before.

'Jazz, please be sensible.'

'I don't want to be sensible,' she assured him in the same husky tone. 'What are you worried about, Tyr? Do you think I'm going to make a move on you—take advantage of you?' Angling her chin on the pillow, Jazz slanted him a look. He had never seen that look on Jazz's face before. 'Are you concerned I'm going to wear you down, and make you do something you *want* to do?'

'Now you're being ridiculous.' Closing his eyes, he tried to ignore her.

'Ridiculous?' Jazz hummed. 'What am I supposed to think? Am I repulsive? Can't you stand the sight of me?'

'For God's sake, Jazz!' He sat up in his makeshift bed. 'Just leave it, will you? Isn't this situation bad enough?'

'You tell me,' she said softly, showing no sign of going anywhere.

Touching Jazz, let alone making love to her, could only lead to the bond between them tightening, when it was better for both of them if they kept that bond on a really long leash.

'We're married, Tyr. Have you forgotten that?'

'I haven't forgotten anything. Now, will you please go back to your own bed and go to sleep?'

Once again, she didn't move. 'Maybe I'm so irresistible you can't trust yourself to leave me alone once we get started?'

'For goodness' sake, Jazz.'

Swinging his legs over the side of the bed, he turned his back on her and sank his head into his hands. 'We're not kids any longer. And this isn't a game.'

'You've noticed?' she fired back. 'It certainly isn't a game to me, Tyr. I'm a bride and this is my wedding night, but the groom apparently wants to go to sleep.'

Sleep was the last thing on his mind, but Jazz didn't need to know that. 'What do you want from me, Jazz?'

'What any bride wants from her husband on their wedding night: closeness, loyalty, trust, intimacy.'

Not passion, he noted. Even Jazz the eternal optimist couldn't push the boat out that far.

'And friendship.'

He looked up when he heard the break in her voice, and saw her tears, but Jazz had more grit than to fold because he was being cold towards her.

'I want you to make love to me, Tyr,' she said fiercely. Swiping the back of her hand across her eyes, she lifted her chin. 'I want you to teach me everything you know about sex. I want you to show me what to do and how to please you.'

He was so taken aback, he couldn't speak for a moment.

'Tyr, I—'

'I heard what you said, Jazz.'

'So?'

As Jazz waited for him to reply, he could sense her thinking: *What do I have to do to get through to this man?* She had risked everything, her pride, her self-respect. God, what a monster he'd become.

Why should Tyr respond when he was only here acting out the role of groom to get her out of a hole? She had no idea how to handle a rejection as comprehensive as this. She would never take anyone for granted again, Jazz vowed fervently. She had thought she could handle anything Tyr threw at her, but then she had thought she was strong too. Turned out she was wrong on all counts. When you loved someone as she loved Tyr, this was always going to hurt.

'I'm sorry, Tyr. I should never have put you in this position. Of course we should sleep. Sex has to be by mutual consent and not to order. I know that much.'

Lifting his head out of his hands, Tyr straightened up and turned to face her. 'You don't want this, believe me.'

'I'm not frightened of you, Tyr, if that's what you think. And how can you doubt that I want this?'

'Brave words, Jazz.'

'They're not just words.' She stared into his eyes. 'We can't go on like this. What's wrong with you, Tyr? It's not like you to back away from opportunity.'

'I'm not backing away. And this isn't an opportunity, as you put it, Jazz. I'm trying to protect you. Can't you see that?'

'You're trying to protect me by making me feel like the most undesirable woman on earth? How does that work, Tyr?'

'I'm trying to protect you from me.'

'Why? Are you such a beast in bed?'

'Jazz—'

'You probably are a beast in bed.' Her shoulders lifted in a shrug. 'How would I know?'

'Jazz,' Tyr exclaimed with exasperation. 'Take the big bed and try to get some sleep.'

'I'm not going anywhere until you tell me what you're saving me from, Tyr. And you'd better come up with something good, because right now I'm feeling pretty—'

Tyr's fierce growl of impatience made her reel back as he closed the gap between them. His face was so close. 'OK, I shouldn't goad you.'

'And I shouldn't overreact, *elskling*,' Tyr murmured, his minty breath brushing her skin as he held her suspended in his arms. 'And as for goading me?' Eyes that speared deep into hers lit with a glint of humour. 'Why change the habit of a lifetime?'

That hint of warmth gave her hope. 'I'm not

about to,' she flashed with all the old spirit as Tyr steadied her on her feet.

'You know I'd never hurt you, Jazz?'

'I absolutely know that,' she confirmed. 'But as I don't have anywhere else to be tonight…'

Looking away as he raked his hair, Tyr huffed a laugh.

'And, by the way, Tyr, I asked you a question and I'm still waiting for your answer.'

Folding his arms behind his head, Tyr rested back on the pillows, allowing his corded muscles to relax. 'Repeat the question.'

'I want you to make love to me, Tyr. This is our wedding night and I'm a virgin with everything to learn, so I'm asking you, my husband, to teach me everything you know about sex.'

'In one night?' Tyr raised an amused brow.

'We can make a start,' she suggested.

CHAPTER FIFTEEN

CLOSING HER EYES, Jazz reached out. At first her touch was tentative. Tyr was so firm and warm and vital, but this was the first time she had ever touched a man's naked skin, and it took a little time to gain enough confidence to explore him more thoroughly.

When she did, he was a revelation. Tyr was so packed full of energy, her fingertips tingled. He was so toned and fit, his slightest movement allowed her to feel the shift of muscle beneath her hands. Drawing in a shaking breath, she dipped her head to brush her lips across his chest, where his distinctive clean man scent filled her senses.

Her feelings for Tyr were so strong, she was desperate to please him, but was concerned she might do something he wouldn't like. Should she trace his scars, or ignore them? She kissed them, regretting each terrible and unimaginable incident that had carved them into his bronzed skin. Tyr and she were different in so many ways and she only wished she could put the guilt instilled in her by centuries of tradition aside. Intimacy between a man and a woman was often discussed in a community divided by gender, but never in front of an unmarried girl, so the little Jazz had learned, she knew from eavesdropping and reading, and from various media sources, but nothing could have prepared her for a titan like Tyr Skavanga in the flesh.

Instinct told her that what Tyr needed even more than sex right now was tenderness. It was time to forget her hang-ups and think about him. Tyr was still a prisoner in his mind without an outlet for his feelings. Maybe she could help him with that. Reaching her arms around him, she rested her head against his powerful chest and hugged him tight. Tyr instantly grew tense, and for a few moments she thought she'd done the wrong thing, but then tremors racked him and like a dam breaking he clung to her and she clung to him as if her life depended on it. There was only one thing missing, and that was to tell Tyr it would be all right now, but a trite response was no good to him. Only time would heal his wounds.

'You don't have to tell me anything right now,' she whispered with her mouth against his chest. 'I just want you to know I'm always here for you.'

'Just so long as you keep on hugging me.'

She thrilled to hear Tyr's voice so warm and wry. 'It's a deal.'

Removing the robe she'd thrown over her shoulders, he tossed it aside. 'Relax, Jazz. Move down in the bed so you're more comfortable. You can even steal the covers, if you like.'

'It can get bitterly cold in the desert at night,' she agreed.

She laughed softly when they both glanced at the braziers surrounding them at the same time. These had been lit as soon as the sun went down to keep the pavilion pleasantly warm.

'I know you've led a sheltered life,' Tyr murmured as he toyed with a lock of her hair.

'What are you saying?'

'Why don't we find out?'

The look in Tyr's eyes was everything she'd hoped for. And they were husband and wife, Jazz reminded herself, so nothing was forbidden. It wasn't so bad feeling small and vulnerable when you felt so safe. Safe and with every nerve ending on super-high alert. Her thigh only had to touch Tyr's to start trembling, while her shoulder quivered when it brushed his arm.

Where to look?

If she looked straight at Tyr, that was like an invitation, while staring straight ahead seemed absurdly prim. So she looked down as she made a big performance of arranging the covers over her.

'You won't need those,' Tyr assured her, pushing them back.

'But you said—'

'I know what I said. I just don't want you getting overheated.'

Her eyes widened as Tyr released her hands from their death grip on the fabric. 'You're in my bed so I can keep you warm. Remember telling me that?'

Was that really her suggestion? 'I'm not very good at this, Tyr. I mean…'

'I know what you mean, Jazz,' Tyr assured her softly. 'You've already told me you're a virgin.'

'Well, I can hardly pretend to have run rampage through all the eligible youths in Kareshi.'

Tyr's hard mouth curved in a smile as he stared down at her. 'There isn't much I don't know about you, Jazz Kareshi, or that I can't read in your eyes, and I don't want you to be frightened of me, ever.'

'I'm not frightened of you.' She gasped as Tyr's hands encircled her waist as he drew her down beside him.

'Really?' Tyr's mouth tugged up in a wicked smile as he soothed her with an embrace that was both light and warm. His touch was so light, she could have broken away at any time, but did she want to?

'Calm down,' he whispered when her breathing quickened. 'I don't bite.' That wicked smile again. 'At least, not yet.'

She laughed. Tyr made everything so easy for her. Smiling against his lips, she closed her eyes. Breathing the same air, she kissed him. Every part of her was firing at once, while Tyr's kisses were gentle and teasing as he held her back. She was still basking in delicious sensation when he drew her nightgown over her head.

'What—?'

'You're overdressed,' he reprimanded her.

Drawing the coverlet up to her chin, she lay trembling and acutely sensitive. How could she become so responsive suddenly? Just the lightest pass of Tyr's fingers on her naked skin was enough to make her tremble with desire for him.

'What are you staring at?' she asked suspiciously when he pulled the covers back.

'You. I'm staring at you, Jazz.'

As the familiar smile carved a crease in his cheek, she turned her face away from him and closed her eyes. No one had seen her naked since she was a child in the nursery. What did Tyr think of her? How would she compare to all the other women he must have known? She didn't dare open her eyes to find out.

'Look at me, Jazz. Open your eyes and look at me,' Tyr commanded.

Cupping her face in his hands, he kissed her so gently, her heart welled with love for him.

'That's better,' he said when she searched his eyes. 'You can trust me, and you can make me stop any time you want to.'

She smiled nervously. Tyr was so much bigger than she was. How was she supposed to do that?

'You ask me to stop whenever you want,' he said, reading her mind with his usual ease. 'Anything you don't like, you tell me, and I'll stop right away.'

Was it likely there would be anything she didn't like?

No. But she had been ultra-protected all her life, and had set such strict rules for herself that she couldn't help but be nervous. She'd heard people talking about *things happening naturally*, and had concluded that was their way of getting out of having to explain to a nervous virgin that there would be pain—or, at the very least, discomfort, together with huge embarrassment. But Tyr was distracting her with irresistible kisses, and each time he caressed her she wanted more. The fact that he was in no hurry reassured her, and when he caressed her back with long, leisurely strokes, she wanted the sensation to last for ever. Perhaps that would be enough for him.

She had to stop this and trust him. She had always trusted Tyr, and while he had her suspended in an erotic net like this, she was in no mood to distract him.

She'd had no idea she was so sensitive, or so receptive to pleasure. Or that Tyr could make her shiver with excitement and anticipation, just by rasping his sharp black stubble very lightly against her neck. And when his hands found her breasts—

'Relax, Jazz,' he whispered when she dragged in a shocked and shuddering breath.

At first she was too surprised to register anything apart from the shock. They might be husband and wife, but Tyr had touched a most private part of her. What shocked her most was that it was a part that badly wanted to be touched. When he drew her nipple into his mouth and gently tugged, sensation streamed through her. The thought that no man but Tyr had ever looked upon her naked body aroused her even more. Tyr's kisses were deepening with every passing moment, and he was touching her everywhere that wanted to be touched until, far from needing lessons from him, she called upon her own, inbuilt intuition to show her how to respond.

Though she did lose courage a little bit when his hand moved firmly over her belly.

'We're husband and wife, remember?' Tyr's eyes blazed into hers. 'Unless you'd like me to stop?'

'I don't want you to stop.' Though once she'd made this statement, her eyes begged him to be gentle with her.

Tyr answered this by kissing her again, his tongue plundering her mouth in a way that mimicked the act she was so afraid of.

'You're tensing up again,' he said. 'Why? You know I'd never hurt you, Jazz.'

His eyes were warm and concerned now as they stared into hers, and she hated lying to him. The ache inside her was unsustainable, but her fear of Tyr plundering her body was greater still.

'Jazz,' Tyr soothed as he smiled against her mouth.

He teased her with kisses, and then his hands began to stroke and soothe, and before she knew what was happening, the hunger for him had overtaken everything else. She held her breath when his hand travelled lower, his fingers grazing the place where she so badly needed him.

The urgency to have her hunger answered was stronger than any fear she had ever known, and, arching her back in the hunt for more contact from his hand, she gave a soft moan of thanks when he found her.

And lost control instantly. Her world exploded in a burst of light, the pleasure so extreme, she was lost in a sea of violent, buffeting waves, while she bucked frantically and shamelessly, working her body against Tyr's strong hand to prolong the incredible feeling for as long as she could.

She gasped as the storm subsided and, still recovering, could barely manage to gasp out a single word.

'You're very responsive, Princess,' Tyr murmured against her mouth.

'Are you surprised?' She smiled into his eyes and saw an answering warmth. 'So, I'm inexperienced,' she challenged with a shrug. 'I just hope you're not laughing at me, Tyr Skavanga.'

'I'm happy for you, Jazz,' he whispered. 'You've waited too long for that.'

'It feels like for ever,' she agreed. But waiting for Tyr to come home had been the longest wait of all.

'More?' he suggested.

She was about to say no, and couldn't believe it when the hunger stirred inside her again. 'Much more,' she confirmed, stretching out her body like a contented cat, against the immense, powerful length of Tyr Skavanga.

'Why don't you just lie back and let me do all the work?' he suggested.

'Why didn't I think of that?'

'Oh, I think you did,' he countered with amusement.

So why was he teasing her? She writhed and sighed with the pleasure of anticipation as a hint. Tyr took the hint. Enclosing her wrists in one giant fist, he brought her arms over her head, pinning her to the bed, and, feasting on her breasts, sucking, licking, working magic, he drew a cry of pleasure from her lips. What made it even more amazing to Jazz was the way one sensation could travel through every part of her until it gathered in pulsing desire between her legs.

Maybe she could lose control with nothing more than this?

But would that be enough for Tyr?

The answer came when she lost control and he didn't. Instead, he laughed softly as she struggled to replace the air in her lungs.

'What are you laughing at, Tyr?'

'You,' he said as if that were obvious. 'This is promising to be a long night.'

'Are you pleased?'

'Yes, of course I'm pleased.' Shifting position, he stared down at her.

She narrowed her eyes. 'And why are you smiling at me, Tyr Skavanga?'

'Because my wife amuses me.'

Jazz faked a frown. 'I think you'd better explain that remark.'

'Let's just say, you're a natural in the bedroom, and you've been hiding this talent for how long?'

'As I tried to explain, a princess of Kareshi doesn't exactly have the opportunity to express that side of herself as freely or as often as she might like.'

'Oh, so you would have expressed yourself before now, if it had been permitted?'

'Stop fishing, Viking. I'm a good girl. Always have been.'

'Then I'm glad you changed for me.'

'I'm wicked now,' she agreed happily. 'So I hope when you talk about a long night, you mean a long night of pleasure for me?'

Tyr's brow furrowed, but his mouth was still curved in a smile. 'I'm counting on it, Princess.'

Jazz was still floating high on the rippling aftermath of pleasure, and that was exactly what she needed to hear. But had she really thought there was nothing left that Tyr could do to shock her?

One more thing she was wrong about, Jazz realised as Tyr placed his big, work-calloused hands beneath her buttocks and lifted her. He positioned her to suit him with her legs spread wide across his powerful shoulders.

She felt exposed. She felt vulnerable.

She *was* exposed. She *was* vulnerable. And had to remind herself yet again that this was Tyr Skavanga and she trusted him. They were husband and wife, and nothing was forbidden to them.

Tyr used pleasure like a spell to make her forget any embarrassment she might have suffered, and to the point where she actively encouraged him when he placed a cushion beneath her hips. Kneeling in front of her, he lifted her even more as he dipped his head and worked another spell, with his mouth and with his tongue, and with his fingers as she pressed urgently against his mouth.

But shouldn't she be doing something?

'Shouldn't I…?'

'Reciprocate?' Tyr supplied, flashing his wicked smile.

Now she wished she hadn't said anything, though she guessed a pause suited him, as it only made her more frustrated than ever.

'There's no rush, Jazz,' Tyr remarked, confirming this. 'We've got all night, remember? All night to please you, Princess, so stop worrying. Instinct is all you need.'

But did she have the right sort of instinct?

The pleasure was so intense, she turned her head away, feeling embarrassed at the overwhelming power of her response. She wanted to cry out, and moan and sigh. It was taking everything she'd got just to remain silent.

'Let yourself go,' Tyr advised, his tone husky and amused. 'You'll enjoy it so much more if you do. Why deny yourself pleasure, Jazz?'

'I can't take without giving something back, that's why. And you can stop smiling,' she warned, longing to touch Tyr, to explore him and test his responses. But Tyr was too skilled for that, and made sure she lost control again before she had chance to put her plan into action.

'You're just too good at this,' she panted out.

'Are you complaining?' he murmured against her mouth.

'I just want to know when it's my turn.'

'That was your turn.'

'Oh, you're impossible,' she complained, finding she lacked even the strength to play-punch him.

'Agreed.' He dragged her close.

'Is this meant to soothe me down?' she demanded when Tyr finally lifted his head. 'Because if it is, you've failed miserably.'

'That's great news,' Tyr murmured.

Every part of them was touching as he kissed her, but she couldn't wait any longer and took the initiative, transferring her kisses from his mouth to his ear, and then his neck. And when she heard his sharp intake of breath, she moved over him and pressed him down onto the cushions. 'You're mine, Tyr Skavanga.'

'Your sex slave?' Tyr suggested. His smile broadened. 'Excellent. Feel free to use me any way you like.'

'I do like.' And she would. Tyr was magnificent. His body was beautiful. Built on an epic scale to a flawless design. Flawless, except for the scars that she traced with her fingertips—

'Don't,' Tyr warned softly as she examined the map of memories. 'Don't spoil the mood, Jazz.'

That map might take a lifetime to unravel, she accepted. Tyr repaid her restraint with a slanting smile that made heat rush through her. Now she could think of only one thing, and that was Tyr. She wanted to bring him pleasure, and, kissing her way down his heroic frame, she only stopped when she reached the waistband of his shorts. Drawing a deep, steadying breath, she hooked her thumbs beneath the elastic at the waistband and drew them down.

Daunted?

To say she was daunted by the size of him

would be massively understating the case. She was shocked rigid. Along with all the other expressions of amazement she could name. She had expected Tyr to be built to scale, but…

It just wouldn't be possible.

She hadn't reckoned with the demands of a body that had been denied for too long, or her own fierce desire to bring Tyr pleasure. Closing her eyes, she gathered her courage, and, wrapping her hands around him, she felt his warmth and power and virility. It took both her hands to encompass him, as well as several seconds to get over the shock of what she was doing. Steadying herself, she concentrated on fathoming out Tyr's pleasure points and how best to please him. And when he groaned in grateful response, she dipped her head and kissed the smooth, velvety tip. But even that wasn't enough for her, so, settling to the task, she took him in her mouth and laved him with her tongue. She worked him with her hands at the same time, while Tyr showed his appreciation with groans of pleasure. This was so much better than she had imagined, and it seemed she knew exactly what to do.

'Stop.'

She stopped immediately. 'Did I do something wrong?'

Tyr gripped her shoulders as he let go of a shuddering breath. 'You did everything right, but you have to stop before I lose control completely.'

I did that?

Jazz sat back on her heels while Tyr stared up at her. His steel-grey eyes were half closed, and his lips had curved in a brooding smile as he reached up to embrace her. Leaning her head back, she closed her eyes as his hands moved slowly down her arms. This felt so good, so right. Could the fates be kind for once, and give them a second chance?

When Tyr drew her down to him, she sank into his arms with renewed certainty, and, turning her face into his chest, she inhaled deeply, knowing this was the safest place on earth to be. Cupping her chin, Tyr brought her up to face him, and when he kissed her this time she was filled with a new confidence. But though they were close, they weren't close enough. She wanted to be one with him.

There was a moment when Tyr moved over

her and she tensed and he pulled back, but he helped her to relax with his hands and with his kisses until she clung to him, gasping with pleasure and with frustration too. And then he allowed just the tip to catch inside her.

'No,' she exclaimed as he pulled away.

'No?' Tyr queried, teasing her as his eyes smiled into hers.

'Don't—'

'Don't make you wait?'

'Correct,' she gasped.

Several short sharp breaths shot out of her. She clung to Tyr. She almost panicked and pulled away. *Could she do this? Would it hurt?*

Tyr's steady gaze didn't leave her face and his teasing kisses excited her until sensation fused seamlessly with all the emotion inside her and she couldn't think or reason any more. She only knew that she had got past that last barrier to find some new, higher level of awareness.

This wasn't a barrier; this was closeness; this was unity; this was love.

'I love you,' she exclaimed impulsively as Tyr moved deeper and with more purpose.

He stretched her beyond anything she would

have believed possible, but the pleasure was so intense she was lost to reason, so she didn't know if he'd heard her, or if he replied, or if he even cared.

CHAPTER SIXTEEN

IF ONE NIGHT could be said to be long enough to learn how to give and receive pleasure, then last night had been that night, Jazz reflected as she rolled over in bed, sighing with contentment. At some point Tyr had carried her from the cushions to the rug, and sometime after that he had carried her from the rug to the bed, where he'd made love to her again. It was as if they could never get enough of each other. They had a lot of time to make up for, Tyr had reminded her.

'We've only been married a few hours,' she had argued.

'But I'm talking about all those years when I was away when I could have been with you.'

'But then we would have been two very different people.'

Reaching out, she gasped with alarm. Where was Tyr? Panic-stricken, she shot up in bed and gazed around. It was still shadowy inside the pavilion with the first thin shafts of light slanting through the windows. Was last night a dream?

'You're awake, Princess.'

'Tyr!'

Crossing the pavilion in a few big strides, her Viking lover, dressed in jeans and not much more, dragged her into his embrace. 'You're shaking,' he exclaimed softly, keeping her warm in his arms as he kissed the top of her head.

'I thought you'd gone away again. I must have been half asleep. The bed was empty, and—'

'You don't get rid of me that easily.'

'Who says I want to get rid of you?' She rolled closer. 'I have plans for you.'

Laughing, Tyr kissed her. His sexy growl warmed her through, and, remembering his exhaustive attentions the night before, she reached for the buckle on his belt.

Tyr might have helped her with that belt buckle or he might have hindered. She wouldn't know; they were in such a rush. Tearing off his jeans, he threw her down on the bed and drew her beneath him. Lifting her, he nudged one powerful thigh between her legs and took her with a deliciously firm thrust. The pleasure when Tyr began to move was indescribable, and she moved with him, fiercely and rhythmically, and as fast as she could. She cried out as she dropped into the abyss and Tyr fell with her. This was the best yet. And extremely necessary, Jazz concluded contentedly as Tyr fell back and they both began to laugh. Turning his head, Tyr stared into her eyes. 'Why did we waste so much time sleeping?'

'We must be mad,' Jazz agreed wryly. 'But as I'm not in the mood for sleep right now…'

Tyr took the hint and helped her to climb on top of him. Gripping his shoulders, she settled slowly into position. 'Oh, that's so good. So good!' Her screams could probably be heard in the village, and, with Tyr holding her firmly as he guided her back and forth, she extracted the last ounce of pleasure and rode the storm.

'This can't get any better, can it?' she managed later when they were both taking a break with their limbs lazily entwined.

'Why do you ask?' Tyr murmured without opening his eyes.

'Because I don't think I can take any more.'

'You underestimate yourself, Princess, but perhaps we should find out?'

Jazz exclaimed softly with anticipation as Tyr brought her beneath him. Lifting her legs onto his shoulders, he pressed her knees back and took her in long, lazy strokes that she could do nothing to resist or control, and within seconds she had lost control again. 'Stop—stop,' she begged him, laughing as Tyr lowered her onto her side and curled around her. 'I can't take any more.'

'You're wrong,' he insisted.

He was right, thank goodness. When Tyr moved behind her and his hand worked some sort of magic as he moved, the impossible became possible again. Arching her back, she thrust her buttocks towards him so he could see just how thoroughly she was enjoying his attentions, and how eager she was to assist.

When she quietened this time, Tyr embraced her and kissed her so tenderly, it took her a while to notice that the pavilion was filled with the most intoxicating scent. 'What is that delicious perfume?'

Tyr pulled his head back to stare down at her. 'Arabian jasmine and desert lavender.'

'Really?' She sat up, and then realised the pavilion was full of desert flowers. 'You did all this for me while I was sleeping?'

'I stopped short of bringing in the horses to trample the plants to release their scent as you suggested when we were down at the oasis.'

'You're a secret romantic?'

'No need for such a frown. I might not be in touch with my feminine side, but I do know what matters to my wife.'

Jazz laughed and nuzzled close. 'You are full of surprises.'

'I try not to disappoint.'

'Not a chance,' Jazz confirmed. 'But you didn't need to do all this for me.'

'Yes, I did. A bride should feel special, and I'm guessing you spent most of your wedding day feeling anything but.' Tyr's massive shoulders lifted in a shrug. 'I wanted to make it up to you.'

As he got out of bed, she joined him, oblivious to the fact that she was naked. 'Tyr Skavanga out at dawn picking flowers for me? I'll be able to eat out on that story for years to come.'

They were close, almost touching, and with a husky growl Tyr yanked her closer. Lifting her, he encouraged her to wrap her legs around his waist, and, dipping at the knees, he took her deep. Thrusting rhythmically as he kissed her, Tyr made her forget everything apart from the wild ride he was taking her on, and by the time he lowered her to her feet, her legs refused to support her.

'That must have been good,' he observed as he carried her to the bed. 'Perhaps you should just lie back on the bed and recover.'

He was joking. Having brought her to the edge of the bed, Tyr moved over her, and, bracing his arms either side of her on the bed, he teased her with the tip while she groaned.

'You can't do that,' she panted out as Tyr drew the smooth tip of his massively engorged erection up and down the place that needed him the most. 'Please,' she begged. 'Please. I need you now.'

'This much?'

She shuddered out a wordless reply.

'Or a little more?'

'You're not playing fair,' she complained as

Tyr withdrew fully, drawing a whimper of disappointment from her throat. But he rewarded her patience—*and her impatience*—by cupping her buttocks and positioning her to his liking, *and hers*, as he very slowly took her deeply again.

'Was that worth the wait?'

Surely, he didn't expect an answer? She was incapable of speech.

Pressing her knees back, Tyr stared down as he withdrew fully again and then sank deep. The look of concentration on his face alone was enough to tip her over the edge. Her wild cries filled the pavilion, and she had barely come down from that high when they fell on each other and, bucking furiously, raced towards the next inevitable conclusion.

The best thing about it, Jazz reflected when they were quiet for a moment, was the more pleasure Tyr gave her, the more her capacity for pleasure seemed to grow. Her hunger for him was insatiable. She would never be ready for Tyr to stop.

'What?' she said as he stilled to listen.

Tyr had tensed. Her legs were still wound

around his, so she could feel every part of him on high alert.

Swiftly disentangling himself, he swung off the bed and stood in silence for a moment, towering and magnificent. And then she heard it too. One of the horses was whinnying an alarm, while somewhere in the distance came the answering yelp of a coyote's call. Coyote were rare in the deserts of Kareshi, and were a protected species, but recently breeding programmes had been more successful than expected, and hunting packs could be large and vicious.

'Tyr?'

'Stay there.'

The note of command was in his voice as Tyr dressed quickly, but she wasn't about to sit around, watching him tug on his jeans and boots.

'Jazz. What do you think you're doing?'

'I'm coming with you.'

'No, you're not. You'll stay here.'

'Not a chance.'

Hectically throwing a shirt over her naked body, she hopped, skipped and jumped her way into breeches and boots, and burst out of the entrance of the pavilion in time to see Tyr running towards the stock pen. Grabbing a broom, she followed him, as lights started going on in the village.

The pack was big, the lead animals thin enough to risk human contact as they hunted for easy pickings amongst the cattle in the corral. Jabbing her broom in the air, she yelled to frighten them away. Grabbing hold of her arm, Tyr thrust her behind him, using his own body as a shield. 'Do you never listen to a word I say? I thought I told you to stay in the pavilion?'

'You don't tell me what to do,' she yelled back, wrestling free.

By this time, the lead animals, having measured their opponents, had slunk away into the scrub. And now the headman had arrived with a crowd of villagers following. Turning away, Tyr spoke to him, effectively cutting Jazz out. She was invisible again—surplus to requirements as the men discussed the next course of action. Was this the husband she adored, the man who had made such tender love to her?

'Am I allowed to ask where you're going?' she demanded as Tyr, having issued his instructions, headed back to the village without another word.

'There's no time to discuss this, Jazz. I want to get back to order the equipment we need.'

She was running to keep up with him. 'So I'm invisible when it suits you, but not in bed?'

'Jazz—there's no time for this.'

Tyr didn't even break stride. He didn't stop until they reached the village hall, where he could access the computers. She was about to follow him inside the building when he stopped her. Caging her against the door with his arms either side of her face, he brought his face close. 'You could have been killed back there.' He shot each word into her face like a bullet. 'At the very best, you could have been seriously injured. You should have stayed in the pavilion when I told you to.'

'So I'm supposed to hide under the pillows until you come back? Forget it, Tyr.' Thrusting her hair out of her eyes, she made a contemptuous sound. 'If you think I'm going to take orders, you picked the wrong wife.'

'I didn't pick you. This situation was thrust on both of us.'

Her mouth fell open on empty air as Tyr's harsh words resonated around them. Her stomach curled with shame because what he said was true, and everything they had been to each other last night was obliterated in the stinging aftermath of those few destructive words. She'd told Tyr she loved him, but now she remembered he'd never said anything in return.

'You're right about this situation being thrust upon us,' she agreed, relieved her voice sounded so steady. 'And in case you're in any doubt, I don't like this situation any more than you do. How can I, when I'm tied to a husband whose attitude towards women is stuck in the Dark Ages?'

'Not now, Jazz.'

She was ahead of him when Tyr reached the door and stood in his way. 'You will listen to me,' she insisted, thrusting her hands out to hold him off. 'I'm not the helpless female you seem to think I am. I'm your equal in every way. Either we do this together, and I mean all of it, Tyr, the good bits and the bad, or you can forget this marriage.'

A long silence followed, then Tyr pulled back. 'Wait there and calm down,' he advised.

Jazz ground her jaw, but at least she didn't say

anything she might regret later. She leaned back against the door, grudgingly accepting that if she had followed Tyr inside, the emails he had to send would probably not be sent, and right now the desperately needed equipment was more of a priority than her pride.

After sending the messages he came outside. Jazz had moved from the door and was standing a few feet away. She was the first thing he looked for, her eyes the first destination he sought. She was still angry and who could blame her? Taking hold of her shoulders, he brought her in front of him. 'Understand this, Jazz—I will never allow you to endanger yourself. Understood?'

She tipped her chin up. 'And I will never allow you to face risk alone. Got that?' She stared at him, unflinching. 'And now it's time for you to tell me everything, don't you think?'

Releasing his hold, he stood back.

'Don't you dare say there's nothing to tell,' she warned as he shook his head.

'This isn't the place, Jazz.'

'Oh? Where is the place? Shall we wait until we're sitting round the boardroom table in Skavanga?' Firming her jaw, she gave him such a look. 'There is no right place, Tyr, but there is a right time, and that time is now.'

'That piece of paper we signed? It might make us husband and wife, but it doesn't give you the right to rifle through my mind.'

'Coward.'

Jazz had always known exactly which of his buttons to press. 'I'm a killer, Jazz. And I'm very good at what I do. Is that enough for you?'

She shook her head. 'You're a soldier and a hero who was following orders,' she argued evenly. 'You never could shock me, Tyr, so don't even try that tactic with me. You don't frighten me and I'm not going anywhere. I'm staying put until you tell me everything.'

'You think I'm a hero?' he flashed. 'Is that what you think?'

'That's what I know. Sharif hasn't kept all your secrets, so I know exactly what you did.'

'Everything?' he said scathingly.

'Enough to know the man I married is a hero,' Jazz said quietly. 'Enough to know you rescued your battalion by risking your own life. And before you start trying to frighten me off with tales of how dangerous that makes you, let me ask you one simple question: Would a brother who adores me agree to our marriage if Sharif thought you were a dangerous man? Isn't it more likely that Sharif loves you as he loves me, and that he believes somehow, and even I'm not even sure how, yet, that I can help you?'

He said nothing for the longest time, and then he voiced his haunting thoughts. 'I can never forget the children's faces.'

Reaching out for him, Jazz gripped his hand.

'There are no age limits in war, Jazz. No sanitised battlegrounds where only adults hold a gun and only bad guys do the shooting.'

'Don't you think I know that, Tyr? But you have never stopped trying to help people. You haven't given a thought to yourself. You're a creator, not a destroyer, and now it's time for you to think about rebuilding your own life, when you decide what it is you want.'

They were talking as they had years back. They were older and the topics had changed radically, but so had they, he reflected as Jazz's frank gaze pierced his heart.

'Who do you think stood at my brother's side

when Sharif reclaimed the kingdom?' she went on gently. 'Who walked through the battlefield with Sharif so we could learn together what we had to do to repair the damage of our parents' rule? I didn't flinch then and I won't flinch now, from whatever you have to tell me.'

He shook his head. 'I don't have time for this. I only wish I did. I can't halt my work for selfish reasons. I can hardly keep pace with all the rebuilding in Kareshi as it is, so I certainly can't indulge myself in marriage or children.'

'You talk as if you're doing this alone,' Jazz interrupted. 'But you're not alone any longer, and I don't want you to stop your work. I want to work with you, Tyr. I want our children to know the satisfaction that comes with building and repairing. I want to mine your time and your energy, and your vision for Kareshi. I want to share you with Kareshi. Just one small step at a time,' she argued stubbornly when he obviously looked unconvinced. 'And if there's more you haven't told me, I know you will, but not now, not all at once. Wounds take time to heal and even you can't rush that process.'

'You always were stubborn,' he murmured, flashing her a glance.

'You bet. And I haven't changed,' Jazz assured him.

Taking hold of both his hands, she stood in front of him. 'Submit,' she suggested in a whisper. 'You know you're stuck with me for life.'

A few tense moments passed and then with a laugh of triumph he kissed his love, his passion, his life, his soulmate Jazz, and one kiss led to another as the flame between them raged white-hot. There might have been people around, but neither of them noticed. Passion as fierce as theirs could accept no restrictions. They remained locked in their own world until the headman passed on his way home and made some remark. 'What did he say?' he asked Jazz.

'He said a passion as fierce as ours is a blessing for the village,' Jazz explained, smiling, her lush mouth still swollen from his kisses. 'That blessing comes in the form of many children, all in the service of Kareshi.'

'We'd better get on it, then.'

Jazz faked a punch. He dodged out of the way, then, grabbing hold of Jazz's wrist, he strode back at speed towards the pavilion. He paused at the entrance. 'You were scared for me?' He wanted to hear her say it again.

She smiled into his eyes. 'You have no idea, do you, Tyr?'

'No idea about what?' He frowned down at her.

'About how much I love you, you inflexible, infuriating man. You have to accept people care about you, and I'm one of those people. So if you face a pack of wild dogs on your own, or any other danger you care to name, you'd better get used to the idea that I'm going to be right there by your side.

'What are you doing?' she demanded as he swung her into his arms.

'Shutting you up the only way I know how.'

'You can try,' she fired back at him as he carried her into the pavilion.

'That would be my absolute pleasure, Princess.'

Mine too, Jazz thought as Tyr started kissing her. Tyr was exactly what she needed—a challenge—a man she could pit herself against in every way. A man she could love, she amended as Tyr held her close and kissed her deep. Every inch of his hard, toned body was pressing into hers, and her desire for him had never been stronger.

'Now, let's get one thing straight.' Dipping his head, Tyr hit her with his uncompromising stare. 'You won't put yourself in danger again, because if something happened to you—' He stopped. He took a breath. 'My life would be over. You're everything I need, Jazz Kareshi.'

'Jazz Skavanga,' she reminded him, laughing as she wound her arms around his neck, sighing as Tyr kissed her neck.

'I love you, Jazz Skavanga, and I won't risk losing you ever again.'

'You love me?' Pulling back, she lifted her chin to stare into his eyes.

'More than life itself.'

'You love me,' she repeated, savouring the words.

Reaching for her hands, Tyr enclosed them in his. 'Will you marry me, Jazz?'

She laughed as she leaned forward to plant a kiss on his mouth. 'We're already married. Are you asking me to commit bigamy?'

'I'm not sure that's strictly possible when you're marrying the same man, but when we marry this time, I want it to be for you and me, and not because tradition demands it, or the people demand it. So, what do you say, Jazz? Will you marry me?'

Lifting Tyr's hands to her lips, she kissed them and stared into his eyes. 'Of course I will.'

Tyr's kiss was tender and cherishing, but when he pulled back he was frowning.

'What's the matter?' she said. 'Not having second thoughts, I hope?'

Tyr laughed. 'Far from it. The only downside to loving you so much is that I keep on having to make love to you.'

'Oh, no.' She pretended dismay. 'But is that permitted when we're not even married yet?'

'Let's break the rules. Unless of course you have some objection?'

'None I can think of right away. Oh, well, maybe one…'

'Which is?'

A tremor of anticipation ran through her as Tyr's gaze dropped to her lips. 'Don't think for one moment that I'm going to promise to obey you.'

'And break the habit of a lifetime?' Shaking his head in pretended dismay, Tyr smiled faintly as he glanced at the bed. 'You're such a bad girl, you've given me no alternative but to send you straight to bed.'

'Really?' She slanted a look at him. 'I was hoping you might say that.'

CHAPTER SEVENTEEN

THEIR HUNGER FOR each other remained fierce. Would they ever get enough of each other? Jazz wondered when Tyr finally swung out of bed around noon. And that was only because they'd heard helicopters overhead and knew it had to be the equipment he'd ordered.

'I'll be back soon—' He emerged from the bathing tent dressed in a muscle-defining top and snug-fitting jeans that outlined his virile form with loving attention to detail. Rolling over in bed, Jazz closed her eyes on Tyr's distracting below-the-belt architecture, which was currently putting a considerable strain on his jeans.

'Be ready for me, Jazz. I'll be hot and dusty, and in desperate need of your attention.'

'Before you go—'

'Jazz, there isn't time for this.'

'Are you sure?' She spoke quietly and intently

as she stared up at him. 'The helicopter hasn't landed yet.'

Tyr was already reaching for the zipper on his jeans. 'You're shameless.'

'And you're here, sex slave, so get on with your duties.' Easing into position on the edge of the bed, she settled back and rested her legs on his shoulders. Tyr was standing up and looming over her, his leverage perfect. 'I won't keep you long,' she promised shakily as he thrust deep.

She kept her word. Tyr did too. He worked skilfully to bring her the fastest maximum relief. But it still wasn't enough. 'I need more,' she groaned when he withdrew carefully.

'Keep that thought,' Tyr advised as he secured his belt.

'Now—' She reached for him greedily.

'If you're going to disobey me, I may have to spank you,' he warned.

'And if you dare do that, I would have to send you straight to bed.'

'It's a deal, wife.' Dipping low, Tyr smiled as he dropped a short, but seductive kiss on her lips.

Lying back on the cushions, she watched Tyr

stroll across the pavilion towards the entrance. His sexy swagger made her hot for him all over again. Tyr was a highly sexual being and hers to love. What was not to like when the man she married was the love of her life *and* the hottest thing on two magnificent, hard-muscled legs?

'When I've finished unloading the equipment, I'm taking you to watch the villagers fly their kestrels.'

'Only when I've worn you out, I hope?' she called back to him.

'By that time your legs won't hold you up.'

'Then you'll have to carry me to the dune to watch the kestrels flying.'

Tyr laughed. 'That's how I got into trouble the first time around,' he reminded her as he ducked his head and left the tent.

Throwing herself back on the bed, she grabbed a cushion to cuddle. It was a poor substitute for Tyr, but he often made her wait, and one thing she did know: it was always well worth it.

When Tyr came back after unloading the equipment, they made love. It was very different this time as he embraced her in the gathering shadows of early evening. He kissed her gently on the lips as he moved, and it was as if he wanted to take his time to savour every moment, as if this was a precious interlude before everyday life intruded. Being close, and staring into each other's eyes, added a special depth to their lovemaking. It wasn't just a hunt for physical satisfaction that drove them now, but a desire to be one in pleasure, in aim and in life. This was love, Jazz realised as she stared into Tyr's eyes.

'Now,' he instructed softly, holding her firmly as he skilfully tipped her over the edge.

'Those are the only instructions you're allowed to give me,' she teased him later as she snuggled contentedly against Tyr's powerful chest. 'But you can give them to me as often as you like.'

'Was that a hint?'

'If you need one,' she confirmed, moving to accommodate him.

Tyr was so big—huge. She would never get used to the way he stretched her and filled her completely, or his ability to bring her so much pleasure. He knew her body and her responses better than she knew them herself. He knew exactly what she needed and how to give it to her, as she hoped she pleased him.

'What do you think, Princess?' Tyr stopped moving briefly. 'Sinking into you is heaven. Working you is bliss. Seeing you come apart in my arms is the best thing in the world for me.'

She smiled as she used her hidden muscles to grip him tight.

'That's what I like about you,' Tyr whispered against her mouth. 'You're never at a loss for something to do.'

She laughed with him, loving the way they were so close now, and when Tyr lost control this time, he called out her name and told her he loved her.

'I can never get enough of hearing that,' she whispered when Tyr rolled onto his back.

'You shouldn't be so amazing,' he confided with a smile.

'Is sex the only reason you love me?'

Staring deep into her eyes, Tyr grew serious. 'The sex is just one wonderful part of it, of you.'

'Cue violins?' she murmured, smiling back at him.

'Must I punish you for making light of my protestations of love?'

'You can do anything you want to me when your mouth looks so sexy when you talk. In fact, just speak to me, just tell me that you love me, over and over again. I'll never get enough of hearing it.'

'You're in luck, Princess,' Tyr said as he drew her into his arms. 'You're going to be hearing me tell you that I love you quite a lot.'

The sky over the desert at dusk had turned a sultry violet tinged with gold. A big ivory moon hung low in the sky as Jazz and Tyr watched the villagers fly their kestrels. The sky was so clear, Jazz could see the blackened craters on the face of the moon, and the huge dark shadows on its cream-cheese surface. The villagers had been so thrilled to see them, they had immediately handed Tyr the best bird.

'Here, Jazz, you take him,' Tyr offered.

She smiled up into the eyes of the man she loved, thinking how Tyr had changed, but then so had she. He was relaxed now, as well as open and tender, while she was a woman in love.

Tyr handed her the gauntlet to protect her hand from the kestrel's talons, and then passed the beautiful bird over. The kestrel was quite calm as it was still wearing its intricately embroidered hood.

'It's a long time since we've done this,' Tyr observed as they admired the bird.

'Another time, another world,' Jazz agreed. Which was why she wasn't surprised by the weight of the bird on her hand, which was almost literally as light as air, thanks to its hollow bones. 'But this is the prize falcon and you're supposed to be flying this one.'

'They're bringing another bird over. And be warned, it looks as if my silver lady is around twice the size of your male.'

'But not half as determined.'

'Should I be jealous?' Tyr asked as Jazz stroked her bird's feathers.

'When my male bird wins, you can be pleased for me—even relieved that I'm prepared to accept that there might be the odd occasion when a male can prove himself superior to a female.'

Tyr laughed; then someone blew a horn to alert the bait man who was standing on a bluff almost half a mile away. His job was to throw up the meat that the birds had been trained to catch before bringing back their prize to the person flying them.

Tyr and Jazz loosed the cords on their kestrels' hoods at the same moment, and with their keen sight restored, the birds soared high into the air. Tyr and Jazz watched until the kestrels had disappeared from sight. The villagers were taking bets on which bird would return first, but as Jazz stood leaning her back into Tyr, with his arms around her waist, she sucked in a deep breath of desert air and thought, *All bets are off. I love this man, and everything else we have to face, we'll face together. The only thing that matters is that we are together, and so close in every way.*

Excited shouts went up in less than a minute. The birds had been spotted. They travelled fast, and it was only a matter of seconds before they returned. They could travel at over ninety miles an hour, Jazz remembered.

'The male's back first,' Tyr noted, grimacing as he stared up at the sky. 'Small and fast.'

'But caring too.' Jazz laughed as the male bird

she was flying hovered instead of landing on her hand, as it should have done. It continued to wait in the sky until the female had landed safely on Tyr's gauntlet. 'You win,' she conceded.

'Only because your bird waited for his mate before he came in to land,' Tyr observed as they rewarded the kestrels with tidbits before replacing their hoods. 'They mate for life.'

She flashed a look at him. 'This I know.' Her cheeks warmed as her heart filled with love for Tyr. For the first time since their marriage ceremony, she really did feel like a young bride on the brink of a new life and a lifelong adventure with the man she loved.

'And now there's only one thing left to do,' Tyr remarked as they watched the villagers start to pack up and leave.

'And what's that?'

'Make love to my wife.'

'I have to agree,' Jazz said softly as they joined a group of villagers heading for home.

Linking fingers, they walked in silence, their steps in perfect harmony until the pavilion came into sight, when they started to walk faster. Jazz hoped that no one noticed they were practically running now. If anyone had noticed, they were far too polite to mention it.

EPILOGUE

THEY RENEWED THEIR vows in a very different land from Kareshi. In Skavanga beneath an ice-blue sky, where the heat of their love threatened to melt the tundra, along with Tyr's three sisters, Britt, Eva and Leila, who attended this very special ceremony of dedication and renewal of their marriage vows with their husbands, Sharif, Roman and Raffa. Leila and Raffa brought their twins along, as well as their newborn baby boy, while both Britt and Eva were heavily pregnant, though even in the last months of her pregnancy Britt had gone the extra mile to work her usual magic on the party.

The ceremony was being held in the open air on the shores of the frozen lake, outside the cabin that had been in the Skavanga family since that first prospector had followed his dream and slammed his pickaxe into the icy ground. Back then there had been no facilities to speak of at the cabin, but each generation had made improvements, and now it had been transformed into a twinkling haven of warmth and welcome: a cosy nest amidst the snow, with flowers of the desert arranged around the door, and around the wedding arbour outside, beneath which Tyr and Jazz would stand.

'I'm happy to get you off my hands,' her brother teased Jazz as he kissed her warmly on both cheeks.

'No more wedding plans to make and break?' she teased him back.

Sharif's eyes were warm with amusement. 'I knew this would happen before you did, but if I'd said anything…'

'My stubbornness would have held things up even more,' Jazz suggested wryly.

'So long as you're happy, Jasmina.'

'You can see I am, Sharif.'

'Yes,' he agreed. 'I can. And as my wedding gift to both of you,' Sharif said in a louder voice so everyone could hear, 'I am happy to announce that I am going to hand over control of home affairs in Kareshi to my sister, Jasmina, and to her husband, Tyr—my dear and trusted friend, who is like a brother to me. I do this because I know you will both put the interests of our people above your own, and I hope this edict will allow Jazz to continue with the work she has already started so successfully in Kareshi.'

'Just hearing you call me Jazz is a great step forward.' Laughing, Jazz threw herself into her brother's arms and hugged him tight. 'Thank you. Thank you, Sharif. There's no limit to what we can achieve together.'

'I think this might work, don't you?' Sharif turned his dark amused stare on Tyr.

'I never had any doubt, Sharif.'

'Oh, no. You don't do that,' Jazz exclaimed as she moved to stand between them. 'I am never going to be invisible again.'

'Invisible? Jazz?' Eva exclaimed.

The two men exchanged a look over her head and laughed.

'Not a chance,' Tyr whispered as Sharif left them to join his wife, Britt. 'You are the least invisible person I know.'

'And now you're distracting me,' Jazz said, frowning as everyone left them to go inside the cabin for the feast the Skavanga sisters had insisted on preparing between them. 'What was I complaining about?'

'Not enough sex, I think,' Tyr said, straight-faced.

Jazz could only be thankful that her brother had gone inside. There were a few things she definitely didn't want to share with him.

'And I've got something for you,' Tyr whispered.

'Later,' Jazz warned.

'No. Now,' Tyr argued. Reaching inside the pocket of his impeccably tailored suit, he brought out a ring. It was studded with the flawless, flashing blue-white diamonds of Skavanga; he showed it to Jazz.

'"For ever",' she said, having read the inscription on the inside of the band.

'"And always".' As Tyr finished off the quotation he'd had inscribed inside the ring, he placed it next to the simple platinum wedding band on Jazz's marriage finger. 'This is for you, Jasmina—Jazz—the woman I've loved for ever, and will continue to love for ever. My friend, my lover, the woman who gave me back my life.'

* * * * *

Mills & Boon® Large Print

December 2014

ZARIF'S CONVENIENT QUEEN
Lynne Graham

UNCOVERING HER NINE MONTH SECRET
Jennie Lucas

HIS FORBIDDEN DIAMOND
Susan Stephens

UNDONE BY THE SULTAN'S TOUCH
Caitlin Crews

THE ARGENTINIAN'S DEMAND
Cathy Williams

TAMING THE NOTORIOUS SICILIAN
Michelle Smart

THE ULTIMATE SEDUCTION
Dani Collins

THE REBEL AND THE HEIRESS
Michelle Douglas

NOT JUST A CONVENIENT MARRIAGE
Lucy Gordon

A GROOM WORTH WAITING FOR
Sophie Pembroke

CROWN PRINCE, PREGNANT BRIDE
Kate Hardy

1114 Rom LP

Mills & Boon® Large Print

January 2015

THE HOUSEKEEPER'S AWAKENING
Sharon Kendrick

MORE PRECIOUS THAN A CROWN
Carol Marinelli

CAPTURED BY THE SHEIKH
Kate Hewitt

A NIGHT IN THE PRINCE'S BED
Chantelle Shaw

DAMASO CLAIMS HIS HEIR
Annie West

CHANGING CONSTANTINOU'S GAME
Jennifer Hayward

THE ULTIMATE REVENGE
Victoria Parker

INTERVIEW WITH A TYCOON
Cara Colter

HER BOSS BY ARRANGEMENT
Teresa Carpenter

IN HER RIVAL'S ARMS
Alison Roberts

FROZEN HEART, MELTING KISS
Ellie Darkins